Cupid's Corner

♥ **Message in a Bottle.** Retired Pirate wants to drop anchor with girl who's not hard to fathom. Great sea legs essential. Apply Shackles McTimber, Under the Table, The Three Sailors, Quayside.

♥ **Farmer Seeks Woman with Tractor** for view to marriage. Please send picture of tractor. Replies to Box No 9949

♥ **Magician Wants to Disappear.** Glamorous assistant needed. You see me, I'll saw you. Apply The Great Marvelo, c/o The Hippodrome, End of The Pier, Sandybay.

♥ **Tubby or Not Tubby.** Lonely giant seeks big girlfriend. Likes eating out. Or in. Or anywhere, actually. You bring the candles, I'll supply the buffalo. Box No 1866

♥ **Wanted! Handsome Prince.** Well-known king offers his beautiful daughter's hand in marriage. Huge dowry for right person. Apply in person to King Boris, The Palace, Vulgaria.

♥ **Caring Woodcutter Seeks Wife.** Have two adorable kids, but hey! Box No 6537

Kaye Umansky was born in Plymouth, Devon. Her favourite books as a child were the *Just William* books, *Alice's Adventures in Wonderland*, *The Hobbit* and *The Swish of the Curtain*. She went to teachers' training college, and then she taught in London primary schools for twelve years, specializing in music and drama. In her spare time she sang and played keyboards with a semi-professional soul band.

She now writes full time – or as full time as she can in between trips to Sainsbury's and looking after her husband (Mo), daughter (Ella) and cats (Charlie and Alfie).

Some other books by Kaye Umansky

PONGWIFFY
PONGWIFFY AND THE GOBLINS' REVENGE
PONGWIFFY AND THE SPELL OF THE YEAR
PONGWIFFY AND THE HOLIDAY OF DOOM
PONGWIFFY AND THE PANTOMIME

THE FWOG PWINCE: THE TWUTH!

WILMA'S WICKED REVENGE

KAYE UMANSKY

PRINCE DANDYPANTS

AND THE Masked Avenger

Illustrated by Trevor Dunton

PUFFIN BOOKS

PUFFIN BOOKS

Published by the Penguin Group
Penguin Books Ltd, 80 Strand, London WC2R 0RL, England
Penguin Putnam Inc., 375 Hudson Street, New York, New York 10014, USA
Penguin Books Australia Ltd, Ringwood, Victoria, Australia
Penguin Books Canada Ltd, 10 Alcorn Avenue, Toronto, Ontario, Canada M4V 3B2
Penguin Books India (P) Ltd, 11 Community Centre, Panchsheel Park, New Delhi – 110 017, India
Penguin Books (NZ) Ltd, Cnr Rosedale and Airborne Roads, Albany, Auckland, New Zealand
Penguin Books (South Africa) (Pty) Ltd, 24 Sturdee Avenue, Rosebank 2196 South Africa

Penguin Books Ltd, Registered Offices: 80 Strand, London WC2R 0RL, England

www.penguin.com

First published 2001
2

Text copyright © Kaye Umansky, 2001
Illustrations copyright © Trevor Dunton 2001
All rights reserved

The moral right of the author and illustrator has been asserted

Set in Bembo

Made and printed in England by Clays Ltd, St Ives plc

British Library Cataloguing in Publication Data
A CIP catalogue record for this book is available from the British Library

ISBN 0–141–31012–X

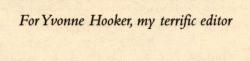

For Yvonne Hooker, my terrific editor

The Cast

In order of appearance

Prince Dandypants – a vain prince

Jollops – his servant, a dwarf

Queen Hilda –Dandypants's mother

King Edward – king of Blott and Dandypants's father

The Masked Avenger – a mysterious stranger

Charlie Tuffgrissel – a young relative of Willard Tuffgrissel

Willard Tuffgrissel – Master of Arms to King Edward

Stuart – a rabbit, owned by Willard

Black Betsy – a horse

Dennis – a donkey

Peasants, townsfolk, etc.

Mayor Tallboy – mayor of Skwaller

Petal – Charlie's pony

A big guard and a little guard

Prince Florentine of Flush – a rival suitor

Lord Lushing – equerry to King Boris

Miss Trimble – a snooty receptionist

Prince Horace of Haze – a rival suitor

Bunty of Kartoon – a rival suitor

Butch of Dragonia – a rival suitor

Kevin of Bland – a rival suitor

Rufus of Ruffland – a rival suitor

King Boris – king of Vulgaria

Princess Langoustina – his teenage daughter

Lady Lushing – wife of Lord Lushing

Bad Bill – owner of a scruffy bar in Glamorre

Gorgonzola – a giant

Slythe – a trusted valet

CONTENTS

CHAPTER ONE

THE PRINCE

In which we are introduced to our hero, Prince Dandypants,
and his faithful servant, Jollops.

Prince Dandypants of Blott stood in his tower room, admiring his reflection in the full-length mirror. It was his absolute, all-time-favourite occupation. He did it a *lot*.

Dandypants wasn't his proper name, of course. It was a nickname. His proper name was Daniel. But when, as a small child, he insisted on wearing ludicrously expensive monogrammed velvet romper suits and acquired the habit of toddling up to mirrors and kissing his reflection, he became known as Dandypants – which, it has to be said, really suited him.

Nobody called him it to his face, mind.

Today, he was a dazzling vision in bright canary yellow. Doublet, hose, be-ribboned silk shirt, shoes, gauntlets, the lot. All yellow. He turned to view his left profile. He turned to view his right. He faced himself full on. He adjusted a curl, stuck his chin out and struck a gallant pose.

'Yep,' said Dandypants. 'I'm saying it, and I don't care a fig who hears it. Today I look fantastic. Fan-flipping-*tastic*. What d'you think, Jollops?'

The morose-looking dwarf standing behind him (and considerably lower down) said not a word. He wore a brown tunic, a brown knitted cap and a browned-off expression. In his hands was a daffodil-yellow hat with a jaunty green feather. He had clearly been holding it for some time.

'Come on, you old misery, admit it!' cried the prince. 'I look fantastic. F-A-N-S-T-C– erm –'

'Do you want this or what?' said Jollops, holding out the hat.

'I shan't decide until you come right on out and say I look G-R-A-T. Great.'

'You've got breakfast then your archery lesson,' said Jollops. 'It don't matter a monkey's bum *how* you look.'

The prince gave a little sigh and gazed down at his servant with a reproachful air.

'You just don't get it, do you, Jollops? How many more times must I explain? People expect a prince to have a bit of glamour, a bit of *style*. It's all very well for you to go round in a sack with your head rammed in a tea cosy. Nobody looks at you.'

'That's all you know,' said Jollops. 'I'll have you know I've been told I'm cute.'

'Cute!' chortled Dandypants, shaking his head sadly. '*Cute!* Puppies are cute, Jollops. Fluffy ducklings and

babies in frilly hats are cute. Not small, brown, miserable people like yourself. You must have misheard. They probably said you were min*ute*. Which you are.'

'Have you quite finished?' enquired Jollops. 'Because I need to start clearin' up.' Glumly, he stared around at the disgracefully untidy room, which was a riot of discarded clothing and abandoned footwear.

'I'm just *trying* to explain,' said Dandypants, 'why it's so *important* to look terrific at all times, because I never know who I might meet. Some gorgeous girl, for instance. I mean, you've only got to look at the history books. They're full of examples. All the famous beauties, Cinderella, Rapunzel, whatsername the frog kisser, none of them ended up with a dwarf in a badly knitted hat, did they?'

'Snow White liked dwarfs,' Jollops pointed out.

'Ah, but she didn't *marry* one. Argue all you like, but the fact is, all the best princesses go for handsome royal guys with great curly hairdos and an eye for colour co-ordination.'

'And pots of money,' added Jollops, with a little sneer.

'Well – yes. That helps, of course,' admitted Dandypants.

'An' a good sense of humour an' a great personality, I suppose.'

'That goes without saying.'

'Like you.'

'Absolutely. I've got it all.' The prince ticked them off on his fingers. 'Good looks, great hair, excellent fashion sense, a terrific sense of humour, a super personality, a rich father and Prince in front of my name. So that's me in and you out, I'm afraid, old chap.'

'Oh yeah? So how come all these posh birds ain't out there stormin' the gates, beggin' for yer hand in marriage then, if you're such a catch?' said Jollops, with a sniff. He began wading about in the dreadful sea of discarded items, picking things up and dropping them in the laundry basket.

'Because that's not the way it's done! Not in royal circles! Surely even *you* know that. There are strong traditions about these things, Jollops. The prince has to ask for the princess's hand. But, hey! Why are we talking about marriage? I'm not ready to settle down yet. Young, footloose and fancy free, that's me, tra la! I'm in the springtime of my youth, Jollops. Catch some soppy girl getting me to marry her! Not jolly likely!'

Highly amused at the thought, Dandypants strode about a bit, then smacked himself briskly on the thigh. It was one of his less-endearing habits.

'So why dress to impress girls then?' asked Jollops, adding, 'Not that you ever meet any.'

'I'm *not* dressing to impress girls! I'm dressing to please myself. Anyway, I have met one.'

'Who?'

'Chucksy Twaite's sister, Narleen.'

'She's six,' said Jollops. 'And she don't like you. I overheard her telling her dolly. *I don't like Prince Dandypants,* she said. *He's a great big silly show-off,* she said.'

'Oh, shut up,' said Dandypants, frowning. He returned to the mirror and inspected his hair one last time. 'Anyway, you're only a servant. I don't know why I even bother talking to you. I'm going down to breakfast. I want to talk to Pops about raising my clothing allowance.'

'Good. Be nice to get some peace for a change.'

'You see? You're rude. And you're supposed to address me as sire. I keep telling you that. In fact, I've had quite enough of you. As of now, you're fired.'

'Yeah, yeah.' Jollops thrust out the feathered hat. 'So do you want this or what?'

In which we overhear an interesting conversation between Queen Hilda and King Edward.

Far below, in the brand-new conservatory, the Royal Parents sat at opposite ends of the breakfast table. The king was buried behind the *Majestic Times*. The queen was talking.

'… So I said, I'm sorry, Lady Wattle, but you really should have mentioned that you were allergic to shrimp. Well, how was I to know the woman would swell up like that? I tell you, darling, these charity luncheons are becoming simply impossible. They're all so faddy. Won't eat this, can't eat that. Poor Cook's tearing his hair out trying to feed them all – are you listening, Teddy?'

'Mm? What was that, my dear?'

'I was telling you about my charity luncheons,' said the queen. 'It seems that every time I have one, someone breaks out in a rash or chokes or swells up.'

'In that case, don't have them,' said the king, rattling his paper.

'Oh, but, Teddy! I must do my bit for The Poor. All those wretched peasants living in that awful place. You know. What's it called? That horrid collection of tumbledown houses we pass through on the way to the palace.' The queen gave a little shudder.

'What, Skwaller? What's so bad about living in Skwaller? Thriving little market town, plenty going on. If I didn't live in a palace, I wouldn't mind living there myself.'

'Don't be silly, darling, of course you would,' said his wife.

'No I wouldn't.'

'Yes you *would,* Teddy. You'd hate it. All that mud. No shower facilities.'

'Well – maybe I would,' admitted the king. 'But it's what you're used to, isn't it? Take my advice, Hilda. Forget the charity luncheons. I'm sure there are better ways of helping The Poor than throwing good food at a load of mad women. Hah! I've got it! *Throw it at The Poor!* There, I've solved your problem. Have a charity luncheon and invite all the peasants. Tell you what, hold it next week, on Tax Day. They can come to the palace to pay their year's taxes to me then have lunch with you. It'll kill two birds with one stone. Now, can I read my paper?'

'Hmm.' Queen Hilda sounded a little doubtful. 'I'm not sure it'll work. They're not used to rich food. They probably have a ghastly peasant diet. Mud cakes or something. And they'll hardly be in a jolly mood, will they? After all, they've just been robbed blind.'

8

'Paid their taxes, you mean,' the king corrected her.
'And not before time, either. The coffers could do with
a top up.' He turned a page of his paper. 'I'd forget all
about it if I were you, Hilda. Leave well alone. The Poor
are used to poverty. It's their Thing.'

'Well, yes. It's just that sometimes I feel we ought to
do something for them. You know, a little pat on the
back. Just to show how gracious we can be when we feel
like it ...'

But the king wasn't listening. His knuckles had gone
white and a dark-red flush was creeping up his neck.
Strangled noises were coming from his throat.

'What is it, darling? Are you ill? Shall I ring for the servants?' cried the queen, quite alarmed.

'It's him!' exploded the king. '*Him!* Hogging the headlines again!'

'Who?'

'Who d'you think? Belcher Boris! Invading Spitoonia this time. Is there no end to the man's ambition? Marching here, marching there, barging in, helping himself to countries, trying to take over the world. He was like that at school, you know. Always grabbing people's doughnuts. Couldn't rest until he had them *all*. There wasn't a tuck box that was safe from him. Did I ever mention the Playground Incident?'

'What?' said the queen distractedly. She had lost interest and was staring around at the pale pink walls of the brand-new, just-built, state-of-the-art conservatory. Delicate cream curtains hung across the picture window, shutting out the glare of the morning sun. Cream-velvet cushions had been placed just so upon low sofas and elegant chairs. She imagined it heaving with disgruntled peasants and shuddered.

'The Playground Incident,' repeated King Edward. 'With Belcher Boris. Have I mentioned it?'

'Yes, darling, lots of times. You know, you're right. I must be honest, I don't *want* a lot of smelly peasants ruining the carpets. I'll just donate something nice for their next jumble sale. I wonder where my boy is? He's very late for breakfast.'

'Simpering in front of a mirror somewhere, practising his smirk, no doubt,' growled the king.

'Now, Teddy, you're not going to start on that, are

you? Because I really don't want my day totally ruined.'

'I'm not starting on anything. But you're his mother. Just tell me one thing. No, two things. No, actually, five. I want to know five things.' The king ticked them off on his fingers. It was a habit that ran in the family. 'Why does he dress like a parrot? What's wrong with armour? It was good enough for me at his age. And what does he do with himself all day? When I was his age, I spent seventeen hours a day studying military history. And does he have to *bound* everywhere? Doesn't he know how to walk? And what's with that irritating thigh-slapping thing he does? And –'

'That's more than five! Stop picking on him!' cried the queen. 'The poor darling can never do anything right around you.'

'He never does anything, full stop,' said her husband. 'He's a layabout, that's what he is.'

'Teddy! How *could* you! Why, he hardly gets a minute to himself, what with his archery practice and his fencing classes and his dancing instruction and his harpsichord lessons … ah, *darling*! *There* you are!'

Dandypants had appeared at the top of a flight of steps. He flashed a grin, then came bounding down, three at a time, like a chat-show host.

'Morning, Mumsy! The birds are singing, the sun's out and I've just fired Jollops for insolence! Morning, Pops. Any chance of a raise?'

King Edward glanced at his only son, gave a sort of honking snort, then retreated behind his paper. Queen Hilda patted the chair next to her invitingly.

'Here. Come and sit next to me. Shall I cut you some toasty soldiers? Or ring for an egg?'

'No thanks, Mumsy. I'm running a bit late for my archery lesson. I just came down to ask about the raise, actually. What about it, Pops? All right if I pop down to the treasury and help myself to a bit more of the jolly old cash?'

'Is my name Midas?' snapped the king from behind the paper. 'No. Get yourself a job.'

'Take no notice of daddy, darling,' whispered the queen. 'He's having a bad morning. King Boris is hogging the headlines again. And the coffers are getting low. You know how he gets. He'll be better after Tax Day. Are you sure you won't have a crumpet?'

Whether or not Dandypants would have changed his mind we shall never know – because, just at that moment, something very dramatic indeed happened.

CRASH!

The picture window exploded inwards, shredding the curtains into ribbons and showering the breakfast table with glass. The queen gave a startled little scream and held a plate over her head. King Edward dropped his paper into the butter. Dandypants dived under the table. When the rain of glass had subsided to the occasional '*pnk*' noise and Dandypants dared risk a peek over the edge, he got the shock of his life.

There, on the window sill, silhouetted dramatically against the sky, stood a tall stranger, dressed – wouldn't you just know it? – all in black. Long, hooded black cloak, highly polished black leather boots with pointy toes, black gauntlets – *and a black velvet mask covering the upper part of his face!* His chin sported a small, sharp beard and his upper lip hosted a fashionably thin moustache. He held a rapier in his hand. He had *style*.

Dandypants hated him on sight.

'What the –' began King Edward, starting to his feet. The stranger raised the point of the rapier a fraction and he hastily sat back down again. The stranger smiled. As you might expect, his teeth were dazzlingly white.

'Forgive me, your majesties,' he said. His voice had an amused, purring quality, as though he were a cat watching three mice paddling in a saucer of cream. 'My apologies for dropping in on your mealtime. May I?'

And without waiting for an answer, he leaped lightly and athletically to the glass-strewn floor.

CHAPTER THREE

The Masked Avenger

*In which we make the acquaintance of a mysterious stranger,
clothed all in black. Demands are made.*

The king was the first to find his voice. 'And who the
devil are you?' he demanded. 'How did you get past the
guards?' Crab-like, his hand moved slowly sideways,
aiming for the bell that would summon Cribbins, the
antique butler. He wouldn't be much help, but he could
alert the guard – or at least bring some fresh coffee.

'It matters not who I am. It's what I have to *say* that
matters. As to the guards –' the intruder gave a little shrug
– 'I have my ways. I leap like a wolf. I climb like a cat. I
slide in and out of shadows. I wouldn't touch that bell,
sire, if I were you.'

The king pretended he was reaching for the sugar.

'The curtains!' moaned the queen, faintly. 'Look what
he's done to my curtains. *Do* something, Teddy! Is he
about to steal the silverware or what?'

'Calm yourself, madam.' The stranger offered the queen a soothing smile. 'I have no designs on your cutlery. I suggest his royal highness comes out from his hiding place under the table. What I have to say will not take long. He needs to hear it.'

Rather sheepishly, Dandypants crawled out, brushed the glass off his chair and sat down.

'I was not *hiding*, OK? I was looking for a button, if you must know.'

'Enough. Pay attention. I bring a message from the peasants. There will be no Tax Day this year.'

'*What?*' King Edward gaped like a fish. 'No *Tax Day?* What are you talking about, man? There is a Tax Day every year. The peasants pay taxes to the king. That's traditional. It's an excellent system and we all know where we stand. Next week, that's when Tax Day is.'

'Not next week. Not this year,' announced the man in black. 'The worm is turning, King Edward. No more will the peasants support you and your spendthrift family. There will be no Tax Day ever again, *unless* −' he paused for dramatic effect − '*unless* you promise to meet certain demands, a list of which I have here.' He reached under his cloak and, with a flourish, withdrew a rolled sheet of parchment, which he tossed on the table. 'I suggest you sign without delay. If you refuse … well −' he shrugged regretfully − 'you must be ready for the consequences. Not only will there be no more money, sire. You will have a full-scale peasant revolution on your hands.'

Suddenly, the man in black stiffened. He raised his head and almost seemed to sniff the air. Then, with another athletic leap, he was back up on the windowsill.

'Off so soon?' said the queen, with chilly politeness.

'The guards are finally on my trail. I need a sign from you, sire. If you are prepared to put your signature to this document, let the flag fly high from the topmost turret. If your answer is no, lower it to half mast. I shall be watching.'

From outside could be heard distant shouts. The intruder raised his sword arm in defiant salute.

'Justice for the working man!' he cried in ringing tones.

'And your name?' enquired Queen Hilda. 'Or are you too cowardly to say?'

The stranger flashed a devil-may-care smile, and gave a mocking bow.

'They call me – *the Masked Avenger!*' he announced. And with that, he swirled his cloak about him, bowed, leaped with a panther's grace out of the window and was gone. Shortly afterwards came the sound of heavy breathing and pounding footsteps as a lot of overweight guards ran by, in hopeless pursuit. The sounds diminished, and once again there was silence.

'Show off,' said Dandypants.

'Teddy!' gasped the queen, fanning herself with a saucer. 'We must review the security arrangements. I will *not* have men in black leaping in through plate-glass windows every time we sit down for a meal. Dear me, no.'

'I'm not signing anything,' said the king. 'Not a thing.'

All three stared uneasily at the rolled parchment, which lay in a sea of broken glass and spilled caviar.

'Shall I see what it says, Pops?' said Dandypants.

'No. Just sit there and shut up. I don't want to hear a word from you. Hiding under the table like a great, girly, cissy, scaredy nanny's boy.'

'I was looking for my button,' Dandypants reminded him, but without much confidence.

The king picked up the parchment, unrolled it, and began to read, frowning deeply.

'Good grief!' he spluttered as his eyes moved down the page. 'Look at this!' With every word, he slapped the paper, so that it went more like: 'Look —'*(slap!)* '— At —'*(slap!)* '— This'*(slap!)*'

'What is it?' said the queen. 'What? What?'

'It's a confounded insult, that's what! I've never heard the like. Listen.

'This is a Warning Notice to King Edward. We, the peasants, have reached the end of our tether. We have had more than enough of your empty promises. From this day forward we will withhold all taxes to the crown until the following demands are met.

You will fix the communal water pump in Skwallor without delay.

You will build a hospital.

And a school.

And nicer houses like we've been asking you to do since doomsday.

You will install proper street lighting.

And a street.

You will instruct your layabout son, Prince Dandypants, to get a proper job and learn to support himself instead of strolling around in his fancy shoes and living the life of luxury at the

17

taxpayers' expense. *Down with these pampered royal hangers-on!*'

'I *say*!' protested Dandypants, hurt. 'That's a bit thick. And did you hear what they called me?' But the king hurtled ever onward.

'*Once a year, you will throw a huge feast to which the peasants will be invited* ... Like heck I will! Have you ever heard the like? *He's* put them up to this, you know! That scoundrel in the mask. Think they could have done this by themselves? They've always been quite happy to pay taxes until now.'

'Well, not exactly *happy,*' said the queen.

'Well, all right, not exactly *happy*. But they always pay up in the end. When I send soldiers to remind them. These demands are preposterous! Fix the water pump indeed! Whatever next? A holiday on a cruise ship?'

'Well, you have promised to get that water pump fixed for years, Teddy,' the queen reminded him. 'Every Tax Day they complain about it and you say you'll arrange for a plumber. But you don't.'

'Have you any idea of the call-out fee?' cried the king, scandalized. 'They're *peasants!* Let 'em use the stream. It's running water, isn't it? And only a mile or so away. They've got legs and buckets. *Dang* this avenger whoever he is! Giving them ideas above their station.'

'It's what they said about my baby that I don't like,' said the queen. 'Calling him a pampered hanger-on.'

'Funnily enough,' said King Edward, 'that's the only bit I *did* agree with.'

'Teddy!' squawked the queen. 'How *could* you!'

'Well, it's true. It's high time he stopped sponging off me and thought about getting himself a job.'

'A what?' said Dandypants, startled.

'You heard,' snapped his father.

'A job?' shrieked the queen. 'A *job?* Since when do royals have *jobs?* He's a prince, Teddy! Born to rule!'

'Well, he's not ruling Blott,' snapped the king firmly. 'Let him find a country of his own to rule. Best thing is to find a suitable maiden with a decent dowry and marry her.'

The prince's jaw dropped open at this.

'Marry?' shrieked his mother. 'My *baby?*'

'Why not? It's traditional. In fact, the more I think about it the more I like it. He can toddle off and find himself a stinking rich bride and get wed a.s.a.p. Then he can buy a castle of his own in a faraway land and come for Sunday lunch once or twice a year. It's got a lot going for it, Hilda. Think of the saving! Besides, I'm sick of seeing him hanging around the place. What d'you think, son? Fancy getting married?'

'Actually, n ...'

'Attaboy. That's the spirit.' The king waved Dandypants into silence. 'Don't look so worried, Hilda. I shall provide him with a horse, naturally, and Cook will make him up a packed lunch. Anyway —' rather cleverly, the king changed tack — 'anyway, what are you getting so upset about? Come on. Admit it. You know you love a royal wedding. Remember ours? You were planning it for months. Years, it seemed, sometimes.'

'Well ...' said the queen, sniffing a little.

'The crowds. The bunting. The souvenir mugs,'

wheedled the king. 'You, the important Mother of the Groom, weeping importantly in your brand-new money-no-object Mother-of-the-Groom outfit. With matching handbag and shoes.'

'Pops,' interrupted Dandypants urgently. 'Pops, I really don't …'

'And a hat,' continued the king, ignoring him. 'Bag, shoes and lovely new hat.'

'That's true,' said Queen Hilda, brightening up. 'I must say I *have* always wanted to see my boy happily married. I mustn't be selfish and stand in his way. I can't keep him to myself for ever. As long as he doesn't forget his mother.'

'Now you're talking!'

'In fact,' said the queen, 'I simply can't wait! My son's wedding! I think I shall wear lilac.'

'Hello?' said Dandypants, quite loudly. 'Is anybody listening? I said I don't …'

'Of course, he'll need to get the bride first,' went on the king.

'How?' said the queen. An anxious little frown appeared on her brow. 'Where from?'

'How do I know?' The king was getting irritated. 'He'll just have to use his initiative. There are all sorts of time-honoured ways.'

'Shall we throw him a ball?' suggested Queen Hilda. 'That's traditional.'

'And expensive. He's cost me a small fortune already. No, he can go off riding in the forest and find a lost castle. Or trip over a glass coffin. Hack his heroic way through a load of brambles. Climb up some hair. Others seem to manage it.'

'True. And he does have good looks on his side.'

'Quite. So that's settled. One less thing for the peasants to moan about.'

'I don't believe I'm hearing this!' cried Dandypants. 'Look, I keep trying to tell you. I don't *want* to get married!'

'Sssh, darling, stop shouting. Mummy and Daddy are talking,' said the queen. 'All right, Teddy, that's Daniel settled. But what about all the other demands? What are you going to do about those?'

'This,' said the king simply. He ripped the parchment in two. 'Masked Avenger, my foot! You know where he can stick his peasant revolution? He can stick his peasant revolution up ...'

'Let's ring for Cribbins and get this glass swept up, shall we?' said the queen brightly. 'Then I shall go and order a new window.'

'And I,' said King Edward grimly, 'shall go and lower the flag!'

CHAPTER FOUR

The Secret Life of the
TUFFGRISSELS

In which we meet Charlie and Willard Tuffgrissel.
Dandypants puts his foot in it.

Charlie Tuffgrissel sat perched on the top of a five-barred
gate, busily fitting a new string to a bow. The field was
known as Archer's Green. It contained a small shed in
which the targets were stored, along with the bows and
arrows. A small stream flowed along by the side of the
hedge. A solitary duck bobbed around in the reeds. The
roofs and turrets of the palace could be seen beyond the
trees.

'I think that's him coming now, Uncle Will,' called
Charlie. 'Unless it's a patch of spring daffodils coming up
early. You'd better hide your sewing stuff.'

The shed door creaked open and a brown bald head
popped out.

'Aye, that's him. I'd best get the target set up. Not that
there's any point. He never hits it.'

'He's *that* bad?'

'Aye. Terrible to watch. He's always looking down to make sure he hasn't got his fancy shoes muddy. But the real joke is watching him trying to fence without getting his hair mussed.'

'Why does he bother coming then?'

'Search me. I suppose it's a Prince Thing.' The head gave a little sigh and vanished back into the shed. It belonged to the famous Willard Tuffgrissel, King Edward's Master of Arms. Willard was an expert horseman, swordsman, archer and falconer. He could do anything that required steely strength and a steady eye. Years of sweaty exercise in the fresh air had made him as gnarled as a piece of driftwood and weather-beaten as an old stone wall. He was so sinewy, a shark would have left most of him on the side of its plate. His eyes looked as honest as the sky was blue.

Appearances can be deceptive. In fact, Willard wasn't honest at all. Willard had a secret. Willard's secret was a remarkable talent for needlework. He had discovered it quite by chance, when a Lady-in-waiting, who had come for an archery lesson, had left a half-completed tapestry in his shed. He had idly picked it up and tried working a few stitches. Despite his work-hardened fingers, his stitches were exquisitely small and fine. Within seconds, he was hooked.

He had persevered with his new hobby, encouraged by the admiring noises made by the few close friends and family to whom he showed his work. His sister-in-law bought him a packet of needles for his birthday. He began inventing his own designs. Soon, he had quite a stockpile of tapestries, all done in the king's time.

Willard began to sell them on the quiet. He stitched huge ones showing mighty battles and smaller framed ones, mostly of kittens and flowers and thatched cottages. Whatever the customer wanted, really. Before long, he had acquired quite a reputation. People seemed willing to pay considerable sums for his work. He had got a proper little cottage industry going. His whole family was now involved, keeping him supplied with materials and running a delivery service all over the kingdom and beyond.

Of course, King Edward knew nothing about this. Willard took care to keep quiet about it around the palace, because he drew an excellent wage as Master of Arms and saw no reason to give it up. Besides, he had a reputation as a hard man to keep up. One or two of the guards might make disrespectful jokes if they knew he was doing something so, well, frankly, girly. The tapestries were a nice, lucrative little sideline. Right now, he was hiding the evidence – frame, sewing box, scissors, twists of coloured silks and so on – down a hole under the shed floorboards.

Charlie, who had been posted as lookout, watched Dandypants approach. The prince had a curious, droopy, saggy-armed gait, as though he would have dearly loved to bound or, at the very least, swagger, but was currently weighed down with heavy thoughts. Like a puppy who wants to chew the rug but has been ordered outside.

'Hello there, boy!' shouted the prince when he came within hailing range. 'Where's Tuffgrissel?'

'In the shed,' said Charlie. 'Getting out the target.'

'Well, tell him not to bother. I'm cancelling my lesson today. Something's come up.'

'Tell him yourself,' said Charlie. 'I'm busy.'

'Right,' said Dandypants, adjusting his course shed-wards. Then suddenly, he stopped, looking puzzled. Had he heard right? He stared up at the boy on the gate, who was doing something complicated with a bow. He looked about twelve. Maybe thirteen. Roughly cut hair, plain jerkin, stout breeches and a businesslike-looking pair of work boots. Some peasant kid.

'What did you just say?' enquired Dandypants.

'I said, tell him yourself.'

Yes. He had heard right. Was the world going mad? He was just opening his mouth to give the cocky young fellow a piece of his mind when Willard emerged from the shed carrying a large board with a bulls'-eye painted on the front.

'Morning, sir,' said Willard. 'While I set this up, perhaps you'd like to get acquainted with my niece, Charlene.'

'Oh – right. Super!' said Dandypants, looking around in a panic. He hadn't noticed any girl. Perhaps she was in the shed, brushing her hair and getting ready to curtsey. He smoothed a wrinkle in his hose and patted his hair, wishing he had brought his mirror so that he could check his nose for unwelcome deposits. 'Er – where is she?'

'Here,' said the boy on the gate, not even looking up.

'She's my brother's girl. We call her Charlie for short,' explained Willard.

'Ah,' said Dandypants, very taken aback indeed. 'Right. I *see. Right.*'

The boy – *girl,* rather – finished whatever she was doing to the bow and selected an arrow from the quiver slung across her back. In one quick, practised movement, she fitted it, drew the bow to her chin, sighted along the arrow and released. Swift as an eagle, the arrow sped into the blue sky and vanished from sight, somewhere over the far trees.

Dandypants goggled. In seven years of trying, he had never managed to make an arrow soar like that. His arrows always flopped, usually a couple of feet from where he was standing. On really bad days, they had been known to land behind him. Of course, he didn't like people to know that. The important thing was to look good while you were doing it, and he was pretty sure he came across as quite Robin Hoodish in profile.

'There we are, Uncle Will. That's the last one strung.'

'Thanks, girl.' Willard winked at Dandypants. 'She's a fair shot is Charlie. Come to help me out, haven't you, lass? I got a couple of jobs need doing.'

'Ah!' Dandypants understood now. 'Sort of, keeping house, making bread, washing up, that sort of thing?'

Much to his surprise, the girl muttered something – it sounded like 'Oh, *purleeese!*' – jumped off the gate and stomped into the shed, slamming the door behind her.

'Now you've done it,' said Willard.

'She's not here to wash up?'

'No,' said Willard. 'Actually, I got a couple of wild horses need breakin' in.

'*Horses?*'

'That's right. And a cannon or two need stripping down.'

'*Cannon?*'

'Aye. She's a tough one, is Charlie,' said Willard

28

proudly. 'A real Tuffgrissel. Well, best get this set up, eh, sir?'

'Actually, no. Sadly, I won't be having my lesson today.' The prince gave a heavy sigh. 'I don't mind telling you, Tuffgrissel, I've had a bit of a shock this morning. Pops has given me my marching orders. I've got to go off out into the world and seek a bride. I've been told to get married.'

'Married, sir?' said Willard, startled. 'What – *you?*'

'Afraid so.'

'*You're* getting married?'

'Yes.'

'You mean – *you?*'

'Yes, me. Me!' Dandypants was beginning to get a little petulant. 'Why do you keeping saying that?'

'Well, that *is* a turn-up for the books. Bad luck, sir,' sympathized Willard, recovering.

'Isn't it? And it's all because of this beastly Masked Avenger. Have you heard about the Masked Avenger, Tuffgrissel?'

'Is that the one they say is goin' round whipping up the peasants and telling them to boycott Tax Day?'

'The very one!'

'Aye. I heard he was down in Skwaller the other night, addressing a public meeting. A bit of an agitator, by all accounts.'

'He's an out and out *scoundrel,* Tuffgrissel. He paid us a surprise visit this morning. Came smashing through the conservatory window with some ludicrous list of demands and talking a load of rubbish about justice for the working man. He accused me of being some sort of empty-headed, *lazy* sort of guy, can you believe? It's all his fault that I'm getting thrown out. By the way, I don't suppose you'd like to come with me?' Suddenly, Dandypants saw a ray of hope. 'As a sort of bodyguard? I'm taking Jollops, of course, but he'll only guard my body from the knees down, besides being such miserable company. But *we've* always got on, haven't we? You and me? I've always thought of you as a sort of bluff old uncle. We could sing jolly songs and have campfires and stuff. Oh, say you will.'

'Er – no, sir. Can't be done, I'm afraid. I'm a bit tied up right now. Got a few things on.'

The prince's shoulders sagged and he drooped dejectedly against the five-barred gate. Willard felt a bit sorry for him.

'So what's the plan then, sir?' he asked. 'Where are you going to find this here poor gi – erm, lucky young lady?'

'Don't ask,' sighed Dandypants. 'Pops reckons suitable princesses are ten a penny. He seems to think I've only got to ride out of here and I'll see a sign pointing to an enchanted castle saying *Princes This Way. Especially If Your Name Is Daniel.* Of course, historically speaking, that does tend to happen to princes, doesn't it?'

'Hm. You don't want to believe everything in the history books, sir,' said Willard wisely. 'The statistics tell a different story. For every prince meeting and marrying the princess of his dreams, there are ninety-seven point three who drown in bogs or get frazzled by dragons or fall foul of witches or drop off mountains. Not many people know that.'

'Oh golly.' A worried little frown creased

Dandypants's brow. 'Ninety-seven point three, eh? Really?'

'Aye. I tell you, sir, 't'won't be that easy. I can't say I've noticed any suitable young ladies around these parts. No princesses living in Skwaller, that's for sure. After that, it's the forest. Two days ride or more to the border – unless you stray off the path, in which case it could take weeks. Then you're into the next kingdom.' Willard's voice took on dark, doomy overtones. 'The least said the better about Vulgaria, sir. 'Tis a strange land, with unnatural foreign ways. You need to watch your back there. There's no love lost between King Boris and your father. They have a ... delicate relationship.'

'Ah yes,' said Dandypants. 'Old Belcher Boris of Vulgaria. I've heard Pops mention him in a very un-keen sort of way. They went to school together, you know. Pops says you can't trust him further than you can throw him. Watch my back in Vulgaria, eh? I'll remember that, Tuffgrissel. Any more useful tips?'

'If you get into trouble, don't use your archery skills.'

'No? You don't think so? I thought I was improving. Oh well, I'll just have to rely on my trusty sword.' Dandypants drew his sword from its scabbard and waved it about dangerously. Willard stepped back.

'I wouldn't.'

'Oh, come on, I'm not that bad. Are you saying I can't defend myself?'

'Oh, no, no, I'm not saying that. I'm just saying –' Willard paused, tried out a mental sentence or two, then gave up. 'Well, actually, I *am* saying that. 'Tis for your own good, sir. Take my advice. Only use self-defence when all else has failed. Running away should always be your first course of action. But mind where you run to. Don't get lost in the forest.'

'How can I get lost when I don't even know where I'm going?' wailed Dandypants. 'Oh, how could they do this to me? Sending me off into strange lands to meet girls I haven't even seen?'

'Tradition, I suppose,' said Willard.

'But they won't even throw me a ball. Even dogs get thrown balls.'

'Look,' said Willard. 'Come on in the shed and have a cup of tea. You're getting yourself all upset.'

'Thanks,' said Dandypants gratefully. 'You're a good chap, Tuffgrissel.'

CHAPTER FIVE

In which we meet Stuart, a rabbit. Charlie proves
unexpectedly helpful.

It was cosy in the shed. Along with the piles of stacked targets and a huge assortment of bows and arrows, there was an old sofa to sit on and a small stove on which a kettle was humming away, belching steam. There was a table, with chipped mugs and a tin of biscuits. There was also a hutch, containing Willard's pet – a large, muscular rabbit named Stuart. Willard insisted that Stuart was always addressed by his full name, explaining that no rabbit of his was going to end up as Stu. It was a joke he told quite often.

The girl, Charlie, was perched on a stool by the window, whittling away at a stick with a small, sharp knife. She looked up as they entered.

'Hello, Stuart,' said Dandypants glumly. Stuart ate a lettuce leaf in greeting.

'His highness has come for a cup of tea, Charlie,' explained Willard. 'He's had a bit of a shock this morning.'

'Oh?' said Charlie. She couldn't have sounded more disinterested if he had announced that there was a slug coming for lunch. Willard picked up the kettle and gave it an experimental little shake.

'Not enough water,' he said. 'I'll get some from the stream. There's biscuits in the tin. Sit down, sir, sit down. Make yourself at home. Have a chat to Charlie, that'll cheer you up.' And he went out.

Dandypants looked dubiously at the shabby sofa, then down at himself. Yellow was a super colour, of course, but it did *stain* so. He took a silk handkerchief from his sleeve, spread it out and sat down.

A silence fell. All that could be heard were little chipping noises as Willard's odd niece worked away with her knife.

'Chipping at a stick there, I see,' observed Dandypants after a bit, just to break the silence. Charlie said nothing. Dandypants cast wildly about for something else to say. He wasn't sure what girls were interested in, apart from making beds and sweeping up. She looked a bit old for dolls. There was nothing else for it but the stick again.

'Is it hard, what you're doing? With the stick?' he ventured politely.

Charlie stopped chipping, looked up and said, coolly, 'I've a feeling we have absolutely nothing of interest to say to each other. Don't you agree?'

'Probably,' said Dandypants rather sniffily.

'Good,' said Charlie. 'Then we have an understanding.' And she went back to her chipping while Dandypants watched Stuart kick his bedding into his water dish.

That was the sum total of their conversation until Willard arrived back with a full kettle.

'Getting to know each other, eh?' he said. 'That's it. Right, sir. One bracing cuppa coming up. Everything always seems much brighter after a cup of tea. Three sugars, isn't it? Charlie, make yourself useful. Pass the prince the biscuit tin.'

'He's nearer than I am,' said Charlie.

'Now then, Charlene, where are your manners? His highness is our guest.' Willard lowered his brows and stared darkly at his wayward niece.

'Oh, I *see* … We're meant to be on our best *behaviour. Right.*' Charlie laid the stick and knife aside, got down from the stool, snatched the biscuit tin and stuck it under Dandypants's nose.

'Biscuit, your highness?' she said, with a sweetly horrible smile.

'Thanks,' said Dandypants, taking three. After all, he had missed breakfast.

'His highness is off on a journey tomorrow,' Willard told his niece conversationally while he spooned tea into the pot. 'Seeking a bride, isn't that right, sir?'

'Oh, really?' said Charlie, poisonously polite. 'Anyone particular in mind?'

'No,' said Dandypants shortly. He bit into the first biscuit. It was rather dry and exploded in his mouth in a puff of sugary crumbs, causing a rather unpleasant coughing fit and some rather unfortunate dribble down his front.

'I was just telling him he's bitten off more than he can chew,' said Willard. He thumped Dandypants on the back in quite a kindly way and handed him a mug. 'Here, sir, have a sip of tea, that'll do the trick.'

'Thanks,' gasped Dandypants, face scarlet and eyes streaming. He took the mug and swallowed. 'All right, Tuffgrissel, you can stop thumping. I'm all right now.' He dabbed at his eyes and brushed coughed-up crumbs from his doublet. He risked a quick glance at Charlie. He could see she was fighting down the giggles. His face went even redder. He set down his mug and stood up, pocketing the silk hanky.

'Off already?' said Willard. 'Don't you want to finish your tea?'

'Actually, I think I'd better get on,' said Dandypants rather stiffly. 'Got a lot of packing to do.'

'Right you are then. Just remember what I said about not getting lost.'

'Hmm.' Dandypants paused in the doorway and lowered his voice. 'Look, Tuffgrissel, about the forest. Is there any particular trail I should use? Heard any rumours of an abandoned tower or something that just might be harbouring a damsel in distress? Or even *dat dress*, ha ha!'

He glanced at Charlie to see how his little joke had gone down. She had gone back to whittling. Her head was bent over her stick. She was ignoring him.

'No, sir,' said Willard, shaking his head. 'Can't say I've heard of anything like that.'

'What about some mysterious cave with a wise old crone who might give me three wishes or a magic sword or – well, you know the sort of thing. Between you and me, I'm a bit nervous about the whole venture. I could do with a bit of help.'

'No,' said Willard. 'Sorry, sir. I can't help you there. I'm not sure you can make these things happen. Probably just best to set off and trust to luck.'

'It would make a lot more sense to look in the paper,' said Charlie suddenly.

Both Willard and Dandypants stared at her, startled.

'What?' they said together.

'Look in the newspaper.' She looked at their blank faces. 'Don't you know anything? Every week, there's a whole page. Stupid old Cupid's Corner. It's full of sad, desperate losers looking for true love. I sometimes read it for a laugh.'

'Is that a fact?' said Willard. 'Cupid's Corner, eh? Well now, I didn't know that.' He turned to Dandypants. 'She reads too,' he explained, with a certain amount of pride.

'The paper,' mused Dandypants. 'Do you know, I never thought of that. You don't happen to have today's *Majestic Times* lying around, do you, Tuffgrissel?'

'Oh no. Not me, sir. Charlie's the reader in the family.'

'You don't want the *Majestic Times*, stupid,' said Charlie. She caught her uncle's eye. 'Sorry. Best manners. Forgot. No, you want the *Weekly Scandal*. Bigger circulation, see.' She folded her knife, put the stick to one side and hopped down off the stool. 'There's a copy in the rabbit hutch. I put it in there myself this morning.' She went to the hutch and lifted the latch. 'Out you come, Stuart.'

She reached in, lifted the rabbit out and put him on the floor, where he hopped about in that mindless sort of way that rabbits do. She removed the water bowl, slid the paper out from beneath a pile of gnawed vegetables, brushed it off and spread it out on the table.

'Here. It's a bit soggy, but you can still read it.'

Dandypants walked to the table and peered at where her finger was pointing. He ran his eye down the entries. There were dozens of them.

'*Milkman seeks Milkmaid to butter up. Apply Box 4392,*' he read. '*Homeless man seeks wife with house. Apply*

Cardboard Box, Underneath the Arches. Good gracious. I had no idea people did this sort of thing.'

'Pathetic, isn't it?' said Charlie, with a little curl of the lip. Dandypants didn't answer. He was still reading.

'Cripes! Do you think these are for real? Listen to this. *Snow White lookalike seeks dwarf for candlelit dinners, walks, etc.* And this! *Jack seeks Jill. Interests include hill walking and fetching pails of water, so no wimps.* You know, this is all very interesting, but I don't think there's anything here that –' He broke off. His finger stopped moving down the page.

'Found something, sir?' said Willard, who was feeding Stuart a biscuit.

'Now, wait a minute. This sounds more like it. *Wanted! Handsome Prince. Well-known king offers his beautiful daughter's hand in marriage. Huge dowry for right person. Apply in person to –*' He broke off. 'Oh, no! *King Boris, The Palace, Vulgaria.*'

'Uh-oh,' said Willard. 'What were we just saying?'

'Bother! I thought it was too good to be true.'

'Aye. I wouldn't touch that one with a barge pole, sir.'

'On the other hand –' Dandypants looked thoughtful. 'On the *other* hand, do you know, I'm not so sure. Here's a thought. If I marry Belcher Boris's daughter, it'll bring about peace, won't it? I mean, Belcher Boris will be my father-in-law. And both our families will meet up at the wedding, and there'll be …'

'A big fight,' said Willard.

'I was going to say celebration and rejoicing throughout the land. We're talking about a royal wedding, Tuffgrissel, not a free-for-all at the Pig and Trough. Don't you see? It's the perfect opportunity for a reconciliation. Pops and King Boris will be forced to shake hands, our two countries will be united, I'll be back in Pops's good books again and we can all live happily ever after. What d'you think of that as an idea?'

'*I* think it stinks,' said Charlie, with a shrug. 'But that's just me. It's your daft life, suit yourself.' With a great show of disinterest, she scooped up Stuart in her arms and began humming in his ear.

Dandypants turned to Willard, who was still pulling on his underlip and looking doubtful.

'It's worth a try, isn't it? It does say she's beautiful. And she comes with a dowry. It won't hurt to take a look at her, will it? There's nothing else in here. And at least I'd have somewhere to aim for instead of aimlessly galloping about hoping some suitable maiden will just *crop up*.'

'I suppose you could give it a go,' said Willard doubtfully.

'Absolutely. Yes, do you know, I really think I will. Thanks for your advice. I'll be off then. Goodbye, Willard. Shake my hand and wish me luck.'

'Oh, I do, sir, I do,' said Willard, crushing Dandypants's hand in his.

'*Arrgh!* Ha, ha. That's a jolly strong handshake you've got there. Right. Here goes then. Goodbye, Stuart. I'll see you at the wedding, eh, Willard?'

'Aye,' said Willard. Dandypants looked sideways at Charlie.

'Not if you covered me with icing and stuck me on the cake,' said Charlie. 'I'm not a great one for weddings.'

All three − Willard, Charlie and Stuart − watched Dandypants trail off back the way he had come. He paused, gave a little wave, then vanished into the trees.

'What a prat,' said Charlie. 'Think he'll ever get there?'

'Doubtful,' said Willard, shaking his head. 'Not without help, that's for sure. At least he's taking his servant. Someone to haul him out of the ravines.'

'Imagine having to babysit *that*,' said Charlie, with a scornful sniff. She turned back from the door and started stuffing Stuart back into his hutch. 'Anyway, enough about him. Have you finished the tapestry, Uncle Will? The one you want me to deliver?'

'Aye, girl. Put the last stitch in just before he arrived. I've just got to wrap it up and it's all ready for you.'

'Good. What's the subject?'

'Puppies frolicking in a rose garden. I'll be glad to see the back of it, to be honest. Some people have no taste.'

'Hmm. Where's it got to go?'

'To Lady Lushing of Lushing Castle. She's having the place refurbished.'

'Right. And where is this castle?'

'Funny you should ask that,' said Willard.

CHAPTER SIX

*In which Dandypants and Jollops bid farewell to the castle.
They are surprised by their reception in Skwaller.*

'So are we going or what?' said Jollops.

'Let's give it a few more minutes,' said Dandypants.

It was early the following morning. They both stood shivering at the foot of the flight of steps leading up to the great doors. Dew lay thickly on the rolling lawns. The sun's rays were just touching the topmost towers of the palace.

Today, Dandypants was all decked out in green, from the tip of his plumed hat to the soles of his long thigh boots. One green gauntleted hand held the reins of his favourite mare, Black Betsy, who was blowing jets of air down her nose and casting uneasy glances over her shoulder at the donkey standing behind her. The donkey's name was Dennis. He was all hung about with hampers, baskets, bags, panniers and boxes containing the

best part of Dandypants's considerable wardrobe. The bit of him that could still be seen didn't look too happy.

'What's the point?' said Jollops, who had been up all night packing and making up sandwiches. His own luggage consisted of a small sack which he wore on his back. 'Nobody's comin'.'

'I just don't understand it,' fretted Dandypants. 'They knew I was setting off at cock crow. I was expecting a surprise farewell party, with hugs and weeping and a fanfare and a bit of a fuss. And maybe a last-minute bag of gold. Where's nanny? I felt sure she'd come to wave me off. And Monsieur Beaupinkly, my dancing instructor. And Cook, with a hamper full of choice nibbles for the journey?'

'It's the weekend,' said Jollops. 'They got sense. They're havin' a lie-in.'

'Even so. It jolly well comes to something when you've got to make up your own sandwiches.'

'*I* made up the sandwiches,' Jollops pointed out. 'You was havin' a temper tantrum about how many shoes you couldn't fit in at the time.'

'That's not the point. The point is, nobody's bothered to come and see me off. I might be gone for weeks. If Tuffgrissel's statistics are to be believed, the next time they see me I'll be dead.'

'Well, that's life,' said Jollops, with a shrug.

'I do think you could be a bit more sympathetic,' complained Dandypants, sulky now. 'It's not every day one is thrown out into the big, bad world. Goodness knows what perils lie in wait.'

'They're lyin' in wait for me too,' pointed out Jollops.

'Yes, but at least you don't have to get married at the end of it.'

'Ah, that'll be the easy part. She'll be fallin' over her glass slippers to meet a handsome young chap like you.'

'Do you really think so?'

'No. I'm just repeatin' what you said yesterday.'

'Well, thanks a lot!' Dandypants stuck out his underlip. 'It almost seems that you're getting some sort of ironic *kick* out of this, Jollops. I must say I was expecting a bit more support.'

'Yeah, yeah. I'm freezin' standin' here. Let's go, if we're goin'.'

Dandypants gave a sigh and mounted Betsy. Jollops climbed on Dennis's back and squeezed between the mountains of luggage. Together, with long faces, they rode down the driveway. Two sleepy guards crawled to attention, hauled open the gates and vaguely touched their helmets as they passed by.

'At ease, men,' called Dandypants, smartly returning the sloppy salutes. 'Wish me luck. I shan't be passing this way again for some time. Off to seek a bride, you know?'

But the guards were already on their way back into the guardhouse to make an early morning brew, and didn't hear.

The palace stood at the top of a mountain. Morning dew dripped from the branches of the trees lining the steep trail. Far below, the valley lay in a lake of mist. Somewhere in there was the town of Skwallor, through which they would pass before gaining the forest, which stretched to the distant horizon and beyond.

'Off we go then,' said Dandypants. 'Destiny waits. Anything could be round the corner. Scary brigands. Killer bees. Nasty unexpected things hiding behind trees. Foul, green, wobbly things lurking in swamps. But with a brave heart and true, we shall overcome, eh, Jollops?'

'Let's just shut up and get on with it,' said Jollops.

'All right, no need to be such an old sour puss. This is an important moment. I thought a rousing speech would be in order.'

'Well, you thought wrong.'

In glum silence, they set off down the trail.

Down in the valley, the inhabitants of Skwaller were already up and about. It is the way of country folk to rise early. Besides, it was market day. Pinch-faced stallholders were setting out rickety tables in the market square to display their pathetic wares. Potatoes, mainly, plus a few frostbitten cabbages and the odd pile of wizened carrots. The small kingdom of Blott consisted mainly of swamp and forest, apart from the nice, high, airy mountainous bit occupied by the glittering palace. There was little arable land. Food was so hard to come by that swedes were considered the height of luxury and only served on birthdays.

Skwaller – the only place big enough to be called a town in the entire kingdom – was little more than a collection of ramshackle houses with a dirt road running through the middle. There was a depressing-looking inn, called The Last Resort. There was a broken communal pump. A few scrawny chickens strolled about looking for worms. One or two pigs hung around an empty trough. Thin dogs scratched at their fleas in the mud. A band of grubby, ragged urchins were chasing around the market square, hurling mud balls at each other and getting under the feet of a very short, tubby man wearing a three-cornered hat and important expression. He was armed with a hammer and a mouth full of nails and was currently in the process of pinning a notice to the town noticeboard. In large black letters, it said:

The urchins paused in their game and pointed and screeched as Prince Dandypants and Jollops came riding into view.

'Eeeeeek! It's the prince!' squealed the biggest, grubbiest one. 'Hey, everybody! It's 'im! That stuck-up Prince Dandypants!'

Slowly, all noise died away. Even the chickens stopped clucking. The stallholders stopped fiddling around and looked up. More faces appeared in doorways. Nobody was smiling.

'Looks like quite a crowd is gathering,' remarked Dandypants as they approached. 'They must have got up specially to wish me luck. I wonder how they knew? I think a princely wave is called for.'

'Lookin' at their faces, I would have said a very fast gallop,' said Jollops.

'Nonsense. You're such an old worry boots, Jollops. They're only peasants. What can they do?'

'Nasty things with pitchforks?'

More and more people were appearing and silently

lining the mud street on both sides. Surly-faced men leaned on spades and pitchforks. Sour-looking women put down their baskets and folded their arms, waiting. There was a definite feeling of menace.

'Hah!' laughed Dandypants. 'As if they'd dare! No, I shall just ride straight on through and … ulp!'

Splat! The first handful of mud hit him square in the eye.

'Gallop?' said Jollops.

'Gallop,' agreed Dandypants. And without more ado, he dug in his spurs.

This was the signal for the crowd to erupt. Angry shouts issued from every mouth, and suddenly the air was full of mud balls. It was like riding through a brown blizzard.

'*Booooo!*'

'*Down with Dandypants!*'
'*Get yerself a job, yer lazy so and so!*'
'*No more taxes!*'
'*Take that, posh head!*'
'*Justice for the Working Man!*'

Shoulders hunched against the rain of mud, Dandypants and Jollops raced for the safety of the distant trees.

Behind them, the crowd continued to howl.

From a copse of trees, unseen by anyone, the tall, masked rider in the long black cloak watched their hasty departure with a thin little smile.

CHAPTER SEVEN

INTO THE FOREST

*In which there are two arguments, interspersed
with a musical interlude.*

'I just can't believe they did that!' raged Dandypants.
'Look at me! Look at my *clothes*! A brand-new outfit
totally ruined!'

'You should have worn brown, like me,' said Jollops.
'Very practical colour, brown. Roll in a cow pat and
nobody'd notice.'

They were sitting by the side of a small stream a short
way into the forest. Dandypants was vainly trying to
wipe the mud from his bespattered outfit using Jollop's
neckerchief. All he had succeeded in doing was spreading
it around. Betsy and Dennis were standing in shade,
gently steaming from their exertions. Jollops had his
trousers rolled up and his surprisingly large feet in the
water.

'I don't understand it!' fumed Dandypants, scrubbing

away. 'I'm dripping with the filthy stuff! How come you're not? None of it touched you.'

'Well, they was aimin' at you, wasn't they? You're Mr Unpopularity round here, not me.'

'Well, it's jolly unfair. And they called me that ridiculous name again. No respect at all.'

'Hmm. You've got mud in your hair, by the way.'

'Oh *no*! Not my *hair*! This is too much. Get the mirror out, and my comb. Quick, man, quick!'

'Not sure I packed 'em.'

'What?' Dandypants's agonized cry rang around the treetops, causing several birds to take off in terror. 'You didn't pack my *mirror*? Or my *comb*? Are you *mad*?'

'I can't think of everythin'. Anyway, there wasn't room. Not with all the rest of the stuff.'

'But my *mirror*!' wailed Dandypants. 'My *comb*! Of all things to leave behind.'

'Ah, stop your bleatin',' said Jollops. 'We're still in one piece, ain't we? Could have been a lot worse. And it's nice here. Nice babblin' brook. Stick around long enough and a unicorn might come along. And where there's a unicorn, there's usually a lovely young maiden close behind. Then you could propose and we could all go home. Fancy a drink?' He took a small flask from his pocket and unscrewed the top.

'What is it?'

'My own concoction. I call it Dwarf's Delight. Blackberry juice, freshly squeezed lemons and pulped apricot. Plus a dash of somethin' rather special.'

'Which is?'

'Soy sauce. I love it, I do. It's a Dwarf Thing.'

'I'll pass,' said Dandypants.

'Suit yourself. Here's mud in your eye.'

Jollops took a hefty swig, then replaced the cap and tucked the flask away again.

'You did that on purpose, didn't you?' accused Dandypants, after a short pause.

'Did what?'

'That whole thing with the drink. So that you could say here's mud in your eye. That was supposed to be funny, was it? Take my advice, Jollops. Don't try to be humorous. It doesn't suit you.'

'Well, that's what you think,' said Jollops. 'I'll have you know I've been called droll many a time.'

Dandypants gave up on the mud removal. It was hopeless. His cloak, which had born the brunt of the mud-slinging, looked as though it was suffering from some ghastly disease. His lovely green hat was so slimy that it could have been marinating for decades in some primeval bog. Plus, the feather was broken. He stood up crossly.

'Come on. Maybe I can brush it off when it's dry. I'd change if there was time, but I suppose we'd better put a few miles between us and Skwaller. I don't trust those peasants. They might come creeping up on us and try to finish the job by laddering my hose or something. Get your great clodhoppers out of that water and let's go.'

Rather regretfully, Jollops removed his huge feet from the stream and reached for his boots.

It really was rather pleasant riding along in the forest. Birds sang sweetly from the branches. Butterflies flitted about in the shafts of sunlight that filtered through the trees. Occasionally, rabbits hopped across the trail. Squirrels chittered at them from on high. Betsy picked up her heels and trotted along at a brisk pace. Dennis lumbered along behind, tail flicking the flies away. After an hour or so, even Dandypants began to feel better about things.

'What d'you think, Jollops?' he shouted over his shoulder. 'Shall we sing? Know any jolly wayfaring songs to help us on our way? Keep the spirits up sort of thing?'

Jollops thought about this.

'I know one,' he admitted. 'It's a dwarf song. I learnt it at my old mum's knee.'

'Excellent. What's it called?'

'I just told you. "I Learnt It at My Old Mum's Knee". It goes, *I learnt it at my old mum's knee, this song I'll ne'er forget. Dee dumbdy dumbdy dumbdy dee* — actually, I've forgotten the verse. But the chorus is quite catchy.'

'Go on then. Give it a blast.'

'*I learnt it at my old mum's knee, my old mum's knee, my old mum's knee, I learnt it at my old mum's knee, my old ...*'

'Yes, yes, I think I've got the general gist. How does the tune go?'

'That was it.'

'Eh? But you just spoke it.'

'That's how dwarfs sing. We're not very tuneful.'

'Well, correct me if I'm wrong, but I always thought you dwarfs were well-known for singing. All those jolly, rousing songs about coming home from the mine.'

'That's a myth,' said Jollops. 'We're a miserable lot, mostly.'

53

'Really?' said Dandypants, raising an eyebrow. 'I never would have believed it.'

'Oh yeah. I'm a throwback. In dwarf circles, I'm considered a right laugh.'

'You don't say?'

'Yeah. Dwarfs are short on humour, as a rule. "My Old Mum's Knee" is one of our more upbeat numbers. I take it you didn't like it.'

'I most certainly did not. No, I had in mind something rather more cheerful, with a proper swing to it. How about "The Handsome Prince Did A-Riding Go?"'

'Never heard of it.'

'Well, you've got a real treat in store.' Dandypants cleared his throat and burst into song.

'*The handsome prince did a-riding go, with his trusty sword and his old banjo, with a fa-la-la-la-la and away we go* — come on, Jollops, it's very easy — *and a fa-la-la-la-dinkum fido. There never was such a stirring sight ...*'

And on they rode, deeper and deeper into the forest, Prince Dandypants's reedy tenor striking fear into the hearts of woodland creatures for miles around.

They stopped for a break at midday. The spot they chose was a sun-speckled glade slightly off the trail, with a natural spring falling into a rather picturesque rock pool. There was a handy log for sitting on and a patch of grass for Betsy and Dennis to nibble.

'Mmm,' said Dandypants, scooping a handful of icy water into his mouth. 'Golly, that's good. All that singing made my throat sore.'

'And my head,' said Jollops, unloading the various bags, baskets, hampers and panniers from Dennis, who kicked up his heels in relief.

'Oh, lighten up, Jollops, do!' cried Dandypants. He strode around a bit, flexing his stiff limbs and trying to breath healthily. The patches of mud had now dried off. His clothing felt a bit stiff, but that was infinitely better than cold and wet. 'All right, so we got off to a bad start, but, personally, I'm feeling pretty good about things right now. There's a lot to be said for the outdoor life, you know. Surrounded by nature in the raw. Good fresh air. Makes a chap ravenous. How about a sandwich?'

There was a long pause.

'Ah,' said Jollops.

'What?' said Dandypants sharply. 'Ah, what?'

'Ah I've forgotten the sandwiches,' admitted Jollops.

'*All* of them?'

'How can I put this? Yes.'

'Oh, *bother*!' Dandypants clutched his head and kicked the trunk of the nearest tree with his booted foot. 'Jollops, you are the worst servant in the entire world, do you know that? You're rotten company and jolly rude and you never call me sire and you didn't pack my comb and now you've gone and forgotten *lunch*! Well, that's it. You're jolly-well fired.'

'Yeah, yeah.'

'I mean it this time.'

'You've got to give me three weeks' notice,' said Jollops. 'It's in my contract. And a bag o' gold to show there's no ill feelin'.'

'There's loads of ill feeling! There's enough ill feeling

to fill a doctor's waiting room for the next ten years! How could you forget the *sandwiches*?'

'I had a lot to do,' said Jollops, with a shrug. 'I had to pack my own stuff as well as yours.'

'You don't *have* any stuff, Jollops. Unless you're referring to what's stored in your pathetic little sack.' He aimed a kick at the said sack, which was currently lying on the grass. His brow creased in pain and he hopped about for a moment, clutching his boot. 'Ouch! What have you in there, rocks?'

'Stuff,' said Jollops shortly. He snatched up the sack and hugged it to him. 'Look, all right. So I forgot the sandwiches. But you wouldn't have liked 'em anyway. They was dwarf sandwiches.'

'What – small?'

'No. Jam and soy sauce. Like I said, soy sauce …'

' … is a dwarf thing,' finished Dandypants tiredly. 'Yes, I remember.'

Crossly, he flopped down on the log. He buried his face in his hands for a moment or two. Betsy and Dennis could be heard moving among the trees. The crystal spring trickled. A blackbird sang overhead.

'All right,' he said finally, sitting back. 'All right. Just this once, I'm going to let it pass. Despite everything, I'm feeling in a forgiving mood. Besides, I shall need you to make up the fire and fetch water and see to the animals and stand watch and so on when we make camp tonight. As well as finding us something to eat.'

'You're all heart,' said Jollops.

'I know. There's something about being out in the wilds of nature that brings out the best in me, have you noticed? You know, this really is a very pleasant spot. See those pretty blue flowers over there? I think I'll pick a bunch. I could present them to the princess. Girls like flowers, don't they? I bet she'd love it if I turned up with a bouquet.'

'Good idea,' said Jollops, settling his back against a tree. 'I'll catch forty winks while you do that.'

'Oh no you won't. You'll scout about and find food for our supper tonight.

'Like what?'

'I don't know, do I? Whatever you can rustle up. Just make sure you stay in sight of the path. Tuffgrissel was most insistent about that. And keep your eye on the luggage. Whatever happens, don't get lost.'

And that was how they parted.

CHAPTER EIGHT

THE MEETING

In which the Masked Avenger gives a triumphant speech and gains control over the peasants.

Time now to leave Dandypants and Jollops and move on a few hours.

Night had fallen, and Skwaller market square was packed solid. Torches flickered on a sea of faces. Everyone was there, from the smallest, noisiest baby to the oldest, most doddery, straw-hatted senior citizen. All the local townsfolk were present – the pie man, the smith, the cobbler, the barber. There were milkmaids and goose girls and donkey drovers. Farmers and peasants had come flocking from the outlying villages and hamlets – Hay-on-Sty, Mulching in the Marsh and Small Oozings. There was an air of great excitement and expectancy.

Mayor Tallboy stood holding his clipboard, waiting for the latecomers to arrive. Those who could read held important positions in the peasant community – not least

Mayor Tallboy, who had slowly and agonizingly fought his way through all the Jackie and Jill readers, and felt he was entitled to don a three-cornered hat and gilt chain, and to hold forth from time to time.

Right now, he stood centre stage; if you could call a few planks laid over a few barrels a stage. He gave a fussy little cough and rose to his tiptoes. Sadly, he was on the lower side of short without having the distinction of being an actual dwarf. He had a squeaky voice too. As you might expect, he had been bullied as a child, which is why he had spent so much time in the company of Jackie, Jill and Jumpy, their annoying dog.

'Order!' squeaked Mayor Tallboy. 'And that's an order. Somebody quieten that baby. Nathan Hogswill, get that sheep out of here, where d'you think you are, at home? Seth Strawsucker, kindly remove Buttercup! I don't care if she *does* need milking. This is a public meeting. No animals, it said on the poster. I take it you all read the poster?'

'Not us,' protested the crowd, who were mostly non-readers. 'Us carnt read, remember?'

'Well, all right then, you heard it on the grapevine.'

'Us carnt grow grapes 'round 'ere. Wrong soil conditions!' shouted a voice. 'You'd think you'd 'ave known that, with all your book larnin', Tallboy!'

There was a loud murmur of agreement.

'Let's stick to the point, shall we?' said Mayor Tallboy firmly. He hadn't reached the position he was in today without learning how to handle hecklers. 'This is a protest meeting and we're here to protest, not discuss agricultural issues.'

'Us baint 'ere to listen to you neither!' shouted another voice. 'Us wants to 'ear *'im!* That there Marsked Avenger!'

'*The Marsked Avenger!*' squealed the oldest urchin, quite beside himself. 'The *Marsked Avenger's comin' again! Oooh!*' His friends danced about and thumped each other, delirious with joy.

'That's right, young Tommy Tinker. The Masked Avenger. That's what he calls himself. Although —' Mayor Tallboy lowered his squeaky voice to the approximation of a thrilling hiss — 'although, who he really is we may never know.'

'Whoever 'e be, 'e'm 'ere to save us!' shouted a farmer with a straw in his mouth. From all around rose more enthusiastic cries.

'Arr! 'E'll tell us what to do!'

''E'll see we get the pump fixed!'

''E'll get things movin' 'round 'ere!'

'Justice for the Working Man! That be his motto.'

'And Woman,' chipped in the woman with the smallest, noisiest baby. 'He supports the Working Woman too. Or he'd better.'

This brought a round of applause from the mothers, milkmaids and goose girls present.

'Well spoken, good wife!' came ringing tones from behind them. 'Justice For All! Never let it be said that the Masked Avenger excludes the fair sex.'

There was a united gasp. Everyone's head swivelled around – and there he was, leaning casually up against the wall of The Last Resort, hand on the pommel of his sword, eyes glittering behind the mask and white teeth flashing in the moonlight.

'The Marsked Avenger!' came the awed murmur. 'E'm 'ere!'

The crowd parted, nudging each other and whispering as he strode between them. The goose girls and milkmaids perked up considerably as he stepped on to the stage. He towered over Mayor Tallboy, who shrank by several centimetres.

'Ah,' said Mayor Tallboy. 'Excellent, excellent. I was just calling the meeting to order. Anything I can get you? Glass of water? Flip chart? No? Well, in that case I'll leave you to it. Ladies and gents, once again, for the second week in a row. I give you … The Masked Avenger! Lets give him a real Skwallid welcome.'

And with that, the mayor scuttled from the stage. He knew when he was outclassed.

The Masked Avenger really knew how to work the audience. He stayed quite, quite still. He waited until the cheers died away. Then he waited some more, until the tension was at breaking point. Then, finally, he began to speak.

'Comrades,' he said, 'we meet again. The last time I spoke with you, you told me the few, simple things that would make a difference to your pitiful lives. A hospital. A school. A working pump. Basic, human requirements that any king worth his salt would provide. This morning, as promised, I presented a list of your demands to King Edward. If he agreed to them, the arrangement was that the flag would fly from the top mast. If not, it would be lowered. I have to report that the flag is flying at half mast. The king's answer is no. There will be no concessions. Tax Day will go ahead as usual.'

At this, a furious outcry erupted. The Masked Avenger waited for the hubbub to die down before he spoke again.

'So. Answer me this. Are you angry?'

'*Arr!*' roared the crowd.

'Very, *very* angry?'

'*Arr! Us is flippin' furious!*'

'Will you allow this sorry state of affairs to continue?'

'*No!*' roared the crowd, enjoying themselves. These questions were *easy*.

'Shall the royal family continue to live off the fat of the land while you, their subjects, toil under the yolk of oppression?'

'*No! No! No!*'

The Masked Avenger held up a black gloved hand. The babble of voices died away. All eyes were on him.

'So. Tell me. What shall be done?'

Ahh. That was the thing. It was all very well having a good moan, but what could you do? When it came to the bottom line, the king was the one with the soldiers. In the end, you always had to stump up. The crowd shuffled and looked at each other sideways.

'You don't know, do you?' The crowd hung their heads. No. They didn't. 'But then – why should you? Honest, hard-working country folk that you are. What do you know of protest?'

'Us threw mud balls at Prince Dandypants,' volunteered the pie man.

'So you did, my good fellow, so you did. And throwing mud balls is *good*. But it takes more than that to start a revolution. Fear not. I will teach you what you need to know.' Dramatically, he drew his rapier and held it aloft. 'You have the Masked Avenger on your side!'

'Hooray!' cheered the crowd.

'Put your trust in me and I will lead you! Yes, lad? You have a question?'

A spotty youth in dungarees was frantically waving his hand in the air.

'Can us riot? Storm the palace gates wiv dirty great flamin' torches n' that?'

'All in good time, lad. Gate-storming is advanced stuff. We shall work up to that. No, I have in mind something a little easier to begin with. We need to send the king a symbolic message, to show that we mean business.'

The crowd stared sideways at each other. A symbolic message. *Symbolic*. It sounded good, but what did it mean?

'What, like in joined-up writin'?' enquired a doubtful voice.

'No. Rather more, shall we say, hands-on than that. Now, listen. Here is what you must do.'

And slowly, in clear, measured tones, the Masked Avenger told them exactly what they must do.

CHAPTER NINE

LOST AND FOUND

In which Dandypants and Jollops are briefly reunited before their world turns upside down.

The forest was dark and echoing – and Dandypants, of course, was lost. There he was, all alone in the dark, and feeling extremely nervous.

'Halloo?' shouted Dandypants, for the ninety-ninth time. 'Jollops? Can you hear me? Answer me, man!'

The only reply was the distant hoot of a barn owl.

Thin, cold moonlight filtered down through the branches of the ghostly trees. They were definitely crowding in on him, he was quite sure of it. How could this have happened? The sun had been shining and everything had been just hunky dory when he had set off on his flower-picking quest. Perhaps he had gone a little further than he had intended, but not that far, surely? Down a grassy bank, around a patch of thorny underbrush, under a fallen tree and over a small stream, then up the bank on the other side, then down again to a mossy hollow, where the bluebells grew in profusion. He had picked a lovely big bunch. Then, lulled by the heat of the afternoon sun, he had taken off his cloak, spread it out beneath the branches of a chestnut tree, sat down and closed his eyes for a moment.

He had awoken to find himself in almost total darkness, limbs numb with the chill night air and head resting on a bunch of squashed bluebells. He had crawled out from beneath the tree, climbed to his feet and stared blearily around, horribly aware that he had lost his bearings. It was anybody's guess in which direction lay the original glade. He couldn't hear Betsy or Dennis. He could hardly see his own hand in front of his face.

The forest was a very different place at night. It was deeply unsettling. The sort of place where wicked witches might live in ruined cottages. Or where ghosts might walk. Or where woodcutter's scary second wives might come to dump unwanted step-children. Or where wolves stood on their hind legs and ...

Brrrrrr.

He didn't want to think about wolves. Best get moving.

For what seemed like an eternity, he had blundered about in aimless circles, crashing into trees and hacking at brambles with his sword and stumbling through thickets and falling over half-hidden roots. He hadn't a clue where he was going, but it seemed to make sense to keep moving. Whenever he stopped to get his breath, he had the sense that he was being watched. There were small rustlings and scuttlings, and the occasional blink of a yellow eye.

Right now, he was standing in a small, moonlit clearing and he didn't like it. The moonlight held a deceptive brightness. Things looked too real, yet unreal at the same time. The shadows were too black. Something ran up a tree and squeaked, then was silent. The owl hooted again, further off this time.

'Jollops?' he called, for the hundredth time. His voice echoed eerily around the treetops. 'Jollops, where are you? Halloooooo?'

No reply.

'Right, that's it then, this time you really are jolly well fired!'

No reply.

'I mean it!'

Still no reply.

'Oh, crikey,' sighed Dandypants. 'Now what?'

Close to, a branch snapped.

Dandypants's head whipped towards the sound. He waved his sword around a bit, desperately hoping he wouldn't need to use it.

'Hello?' he quavered. 'Is anyone there?'

No response. Dandypants broke out into a cold sweat. His legs felt rubbery and his heart was racing. When another branch cracked, closer this time, he gave a small scream. Whatever was coming wasn't in the clearing, not yet, but almost. There was the unmistakable smell of smoke. Oh no! Surely not a *dragon?* He'd never seen one in the flesh, but he had seen pictures. Oh, yes, he had seen pictures.

He raised his sword. It trembled in his slippery grasp. A little whimper rose in his throat.

And then – the undergrowth parted!

'There you are,' said Jollops. 'Are you comin' back or what?'

In his hand, he held a flaming branch. Great, acrid puffs of smoke blew around.

'Good gosh, man!' cried Dandypants, staggering around and wiping his streaming brow. 'What a fright you gave me! Do you have to creep up on me like that? For a moment there, I thought were a *dragon* come to jolly well *eat* me! Where have you *been?*'

'I might ask the same of you,' said Jollops sourly. 'I been callin' for hours. You was asleep, wasn't you?'

'Well – yes, I did have a bit of a snooze,' admitted Dandypants. 'But that was *ages* ago. What have you been doing all this time?'

'What d'you think? Looking for you,' said Jollops.

That wasn't *quite* true. In fact, Jollops had made good use of the last few hours. He had gone off looking for supper ingredients, as instructed. Quite by luck, he had found a good crop of oyster mushrooms growing on a fallen tree and filled his hat with them. He also found some wild strawberries. He then returned to the sun-speckled glade, where he sat on a stump and waited in vain for his master's return.

When the sun set, he took out a small frying pan, built a camp fire and cooked himself a tasty little meal of mushrooms. He had followed this with a handful of strawberries, a cool drink of water from the stream and a hearty swig or two of Dwarf's Delight. All very civilized.

When he had finished eating, he washed the pan, lay
back and watched the stars come out and the moon rise.
A short time later, Dandypants's panicked shouts and
wild crashings began. Sometimes they sounded far away,

at other times, quite close. They were hard to ignore. Jollops tried to block them out for a while, but in the end found he could take it no longer. The peace of the night was totally ruined. So, armed with a flaming branch from the fire, he had reluctantly set off on a rescue mission.

'Well,' said Dandypants. 'All I can say is, you've got cloth ears.'

'That's rich, comin' from you,' said Jollops. 'You're the one who got lost, remember? Don't go blamin' me.'

The argument would have gone on for some time – but, just at that moment, there came an interruption.

There was the unmistakable sound of footsteps crashing through the undergrowth. Dozens of them, by the sound of it, drawing ever closer. And voices. Angry voices, shouting things. Rude things. Anti-royalist things. Things like '*Down with the Monarchy!*' and '*Justice for the Working Man!*' And then, through the trees came a mob of furious peasants. Some were waving pitchforks and brandishing lighted torches. Others were carrying all-too-familiar boxes, baskets, bags and hampers. The lids had been roughly wrenched off to expose Dandypants's carefully folded, colour co-ordinated clothing, which was now in disarray. A small urchin had possession of Jollop's frying pan. Another was merrily prancing around in one of Dandypants's best plumed hats!

'Uh-oh,' sighed Jollops. 'An angry mob. Goody. That's all we need.'

'I don't believe this!' gasped Dandypants. 'That's our luggage! That's my *clothes* they've got there! Hey! Take my hat off, you cheeky little tyke!'

The peasants in front caught sight of Dandypants and Jollops and stopped, causing a bit of a pile up behind.

'There he is!' screeched a woman in a mob cap, brandishing a rolling pin. 'Let's get 'im!'

And before Dandypants quite knew what was happening, they were rushing at him. He found himself seized by rough hands and pinned to the ground. Someone divested him of his sword, and someone else threw his hat into a tree. Somebody sat on his head. Somebody else grabbed his wildly thrashing feet and proceeded to tie them tightly together with rope. Then – and this was particularly unpleasant – the end of the rope was tossed over a high branch of a nearby tree. Two large figures in smocks hauled on the end – and Dandypants found himself rising from the ground, feet first. Spinning wildly, up, up he rose, until the soles of his boots scraped the high branch. The large figures who were doing the hauling tied the end of the rope to a lower limb, then stood back and stared up at him.

'How's that feel, yer *royal 'ighness*?' jeered one of them. 'Now you can really look down on us, eh?'

'You wait!' choked Dandypants. 'You'll be jolly sorry when Pops gets to hear about this!'

'That's all you know!' said the second. 'Us 've got a proper leader now. Things are gonna change around 'ere.'

'*Oooh!*' mimicked the urchin in Dandypants's hat, doing a stupid, mincing walk. 'I'm Prince *Dandypants,* I am! Look at *me!*'

This was greeted by laughter and wild cheers from the peasants. Dandypants said nothing more When you're suspended upside down in the air with the blood draining into your head and a mob with a grudge below, there's not a lot to say, really.

Something spinning around about a metre to his right caught his eye. It seemed that Jollops had suffered the same treatment.

Below, the peasants had got into a huddle. They appeared to be debating what to do next. Then –

'*Burn!*' shrieked a voice. It belonged to a spotty youth in dungarees. 'Burn his fancy clothes! Burn 'em! Burn 'em!'

The crowd took up the chant.

'Arr! That's right! *Burn! Burn 'em! Burn 'em!*'

'Hey!' croaked Dandypants. This was too much. 'Don't you *dare* burn my stuff! Who said you could do that?'

'*He* did,' replied the spotty youth. 'The Masked Avenger. Us are gonna make a gurt big bonfire outside the palace gates. 'Tis a shambolic gesture.'

'I knew it!' cried Dandypants. 'I *knew* that trouble-making bounder would be behind this. Look, you don't want to believe a thing he says. Let me down and we'll talk about this in a calm and civilized fashion …'

But his protests fell on deaf ears. Already the mob was rushing off into the darkness, led by the fierce woman with the rolling pin. Their thundering footsteps and angry voices faded into the distance – and once again, Dandypants and Jollops were alone. Alone and helpless, suspended by their ankles a good three metres in the air and still spinning.

Conversation was difficult, owing to their differing

rates of spin. But right now, conversation was all they had.

'Jollops?' shouted Dandypants, above the noise of blood roaring in his ears.

'What?'

'I just want to make one thing clear. I hold you responsible for this.'

'Eh? How d'you make that out?'

'You were supposed to be acting as lookout.'

'I was. I was lookin' for you, remember?'

'But you left the luggage unattended, didn't you? And now they're going to burn my clothes! My *clothes,* Jollops. My beautiful, carefully selected *clothes*!'

'We're hangin' upside down from a tree,' pointed out Jollops. 'Now ain't the time to discuss your wardrobe.'

'Then you'd better think about getting us down, hadn't you? Because the minute we're the right way up, I'm jolly well going to give you a piece of my mind. I can't leave you for a moment, can I? I clearly instructed you to stay in sight of the glade. Deny it if you can.'

'Would it be too much to ask you to shut up for a minute?' requested Jollops. 'Because I've got a headache comin' on.'

'Good,' said Dandypants spitefully. Adding, 'And you're the one who should shut up. Seeing as it's all your fault.'

Mercifully, the rate of spin was slowing down. The world ceased revolving. Now they just hung there in the moonlight, glaring at each other upside down and sideways.

'Well, go on then,' said Dandypants. '*Do* something.'

'Like what?'

'Well, you're short, aren't you? It's not that far to your toes. Try and pull yourself up on to the branch. That'd be a start.'

'That'd be a miracle,' said Jollops. 'Far as I know, there ain't no baboon in my family tree. There's only one thing we can do.'

'What?'

'Hang about and shout for help,' said Jollops.

And that was what they did. They shouted until their throats were sore. They didn't stop until the sky began to lighten and twitterings from the throats of a thousand birds replaced the forlorn hootings of the night owls. Then they gave up and simply dangled in miserable silence.

And that was how Charlie found them.

CHAPTER TEN

RESCUED

In which Charlie comes to the rescue, Dandypants mourns his wardrobe and Jollops gets his stuff back.

The bushes parted once more – and she rode into the clearing on a small brown pony. Betsy and Dennis followed behind on leading reins. She had a bow slung over one shoulder, and a quiver full of arrows on her back. There was a good selection of knives in her belt. A large, floppy-looking package wrapped in brown paper lay across the saddle in front of her.

She came to a halt beneath the tree from which Dandypants and Jollops were suspended and stared up at them.

'Morning, boys,' she said cheerily. 'Is this one of your regular hang-outs?'

'Very funny,' croaked Dandypants tightly. 'I think we've exhausted the jokes about hanging. Would it be too much trouble to ask you to get us down, do you think?'

'With pleasure,' said Charlie. 'Here comes the cavalry.' And she dismounted, took a sharp knife from her belt and strode purposefully towards the tree.

'No!' shouted Dandypants urgently. 'Not that way! Don't cut the rope, it's too far to faaaaaaaallllllll .... arrrrrrgh ....'

The sensation of dropping head first from a great height is bad. Landing is much, much worse.

Crump! All the breath was jolted out of him as he landed face down in a pile of leaves. A similar sound a short way to his right indicated that Jollops, too, was once more forcibly reunited with the ground.

Slowly, spitting out a mouthful of small twigs and assorted undergrowth, Dandypants sat up and inspected himself for injuries. His knees had taken the worst bashing. There were two great, ragged holes in his hose exposing painfully scratched flesh, from which thin trickles of blood were already beginning to well. He could have wept. Brand new hose, utterly ruined. He reached up and patted his head. Hair full of leaves, just as he suspected. And no comb.

'Sorry about that, but it was the only way,' said Charlie. She stuck out a hand. 'Need a hand up?'

'No,' growled Dandypants. 'Leave me alone. Everything's spinning. I feel sick.'

'Suit yourself. I expected a bit of gratitude. But, hey! I'll be on my way.'

'*I'm* grateful,' said Jollops, clambering to his feet and brushing off leaves. 'Thanks, lad.'

'It's not a lad,' said Dandypants, wincing as he pressed a handful of soothing moss on to his sore knees. 'It's a girl. Tuffgrissell's niece, Charlene. *Ouch.* This hurts.'

'In that case, thanks, Miss Charlene,' said Jollops, with a little bow. 'Very kind of you to come to our aid. Dunno what we'd have done if you hadn't happened along.'

'Call me Charlie,' said Charlie. 'Nice to meet you, Jollops. You're cute. Love the hat.' She stuck out her hand, and they shook.

'Have you quite finished?' enquired Dandypants. 'Because I'd rather like to get away from here before the mob decides to come back and sling us up again.'

'No chance of that,' said Charlie. 'They've gone back to Skwaller. I passed them a while back. Petal and I were just riding along, minding our own business, and they came rushing out of the trees with all your luggage, shouting about making a bonfire in front of the palace gates. They've got your money too, I think, because they were talking about going to the pub first.'

'That wretched Masked Avenger!' wailed Dandypants. '*He's* making them like this! They've never gone this far before. Oh, my clothes, my clothes!' He rocked to and fro with his head in his hands. 'My new lemon doublet with the ribbons! And my peacock-blue velvet admiral's jacket with the gold braiding and the brass buttons! Gone, all gone! And my money! The bag of gold Mumsy gave me for expenses! I haven't got a farthing to my name now! Have you got any money, Jollops?'

'Half a crown,' said Jollops.

'Well, give it to me for safe-keeping,' ordered Dandypants. 'It doesn't feel *right,* not having any money. Princes are *supposed* to have money. It goes with the job.'

'Oh, shut up,' said Charlie. 'Stop moaning all the time. Moan, moan, moan. You're such a moaner. At least you've still got your horse and your donkey. They had the sense to take off once they smelt trouble coming. It took me ages to round them up.'

'But my *clothes!* Did you inspect the campsite? Is *everything* gone?'

'Everything except this.' Charlie reached over and pulled a small sack from Dennis's back.

'Hey!' said Jollops, delighted. 'That's my stuff! Thanks.'

'Oh, jolly good,' said Dandypants coldly. He climbed to his feet, wincing in pain as his battered knees straightened. 'All my highly expensive designer clothing is destined to go up in flames, but Jollops has his *stuff.* Splendid. Let's all give three cheers. Hip, hip, hoo flipping ray.'

'It seems fair enough to me,' said Charlie. 'It's you royals the peasants have got a quarrel with, not the poor saps who work for you.'

'I see,' said Dandypants, stiffly. 'Siding with the peasantry now, are we? Of course, you're probably from peasant stock yourself. For all I know, you might have helped them do it. You could be a double agent. The Masked Avenger's probably a *relation* of yours.'

'Well, there's a nice thing to say, after she cut us down and all!' scolded Jollops. 'Take no notice of 'im, Miss Charlie.'

Charlie didn't say a word. Her disgusted look did all the talking. Dandypants dropped his eyes, unable to meet her contemptuous glare.

'Well, all right, perhaps that was going a little far,' he

muttered. 'But you must admit, it's a bit odd, you turning up in the forest just as it all happened.'

'It may come as a surprise to you,' said Charlie coldly, 'but even your stuck-up *dad* can't stop people from riding where they want when they feel like it. If you must know, Uncle Willard asked me to keep an eye out for you. I didn't really want to, but I was going this way anyway and I said I would. I wish I'd left you dangling now. Not you,' she added, to Jollops. 'I'm talking about his high and mightiness here.'

Jollops looked smug.

'Anyway,' continued Charlie, 'anyway, I can't waste any more time. I've got business in Vulgaria.'

'What sort of business?' enquired Dandypants.

'My own. And I'll thank you to mind yours. I'm off. Be seeing you, Jollops. You have my deepest sympathy.'

She turned on her heel and stalked over to the waiting pony. She checked that the big, floppy parcel was securely strapped on, then placed her foot in the stirrup.

'You're not just going to stand there and let her go, are you?' said Jollops, as they watched her mount and ride away without a backward glance.

'Yes,' said Dandypants sulkily. 'Good riddance, I say. Who needs her? She's so *up-tight*. You can't say a word unless she jumps down your throat.'

'Are you nuts? You heard her. She's makin' for Vulgaria. She knows the way. We could tag along with her. She's like a one girl army. She's got a proper bow and knives and everythin'.'

'I'm a prince,' said Dandypants haughtily. 'I don't need the protection of some stupid girl.'

'Oh no? And what if we get into more trouble? You haven't even got your sword now. Not that it'd make any difference. Besides, she might have sandwiches.'

Dandypants thought about this. He hated to admit it, but Jollops was making a lot of sense. Despite the daylight, he hadn't a clue how to get back on to the trail. They had no weapons, plus it had been a very long time since he had eaten. Suddenly, his appetite returned with a vengeance.

'All right,' he said, placing a foot in Betsy's stirrup. 'I suppose there's safety in numbers. But don't expect me to apologize. She's got an attitude problem, that girl.'

Charlie was riding at a brisk trot along the trail when she heard the shout.

'Hey! Slow down, will you?'

She reigned in the brown pony and looked over her shoulder. Dandypants and Jollops were emerging from the trees some way behind. She waited for them to catch up. They both looked rather worse for wear – Dandypants in particular. She almost felt sorry for the pathetic creep. Almost.

'What now?' said Charlie as they rode up.

'I've been thinking,' said Dandypants. 'I was probably a little hasty back there. I wasn't thinking straight. Anyway, it's silly, us all riding separately, seeing as we're all heading for the same place, right?'

'So you're saying you're sorry?'

'No. Princes never apologize. I'm just explaining.'

'So you're *not* saying sorry?'

Suddenly, Dandypants felt very tired. It was all too

much. He had only left home twenty-four hours ago, and already he had been booed, pelted with mud, lost, hung upside down from a tree, robbed of his clothes and – the final straw, this – rescued by a girl. And not just any girl. Willard's rude, prickly niece, who hadn't the slightest idea how to behave with royalty.

But who might have sandwiches.

'Look,' he said, rubbing his eyes. 'I haven't eaten a thing since supper last night. I don't suppose you've got any food, have you? Perhaps a small hunk of cheese or something?'

'So you *are* saying sorry?'

Dandypants caught sight of Jollops, who was rolling his eyes around and nodding his head up and down encouragingly.

'Well – all right. Yes. I am. Sorry. There. I've said it. Can I have a sandwich? Please?'

'No. I haven't got any.' Dandypants's face fell. Charlie softened a little. 'I've got some apples though. Oh, all right, you can ride along with me, I suppose. Somebody'd better keep an eye on you. But when we reach Vulgaria, you're on your own. Agreed?'

'Agreed,' said Dandypants, quite humbly for him.

CHAPTER ELEVEN

...AND THEN THERE WERE THREE

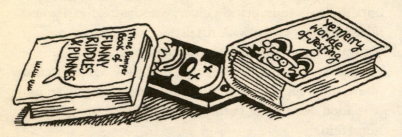

In which Jollops tells a secret and a joke,
and Dandypants sulks.

'Sulking, isn't he?' said Charlie to Jollops, with a nod over her shoulder. The track wasn't wide enough to take more than two abreast and Dandypants was forced to trail along behind.

'Yep,' said Jollops.

'I don't know how you put up with him.'

'I won't for much longer. I got plans for a career change,' said Jollops mysteriously.

'Oh yes?' Charlie was curious. 'Like what?'

'Promise you won't tell?'

'Cross my heart. What?'

'I'm gonna be a jester,' Jollops told her. 'I'm takin' a correspondence course. Got all the books in my sack. *Thee Bumper Book of Funny Riddles and Punnes. The Solemn Art of Clowning. Ye Merry Worlde of Jesting.*'

'Wow,' said Charlie. 'A jester, eh? That sounds fun.'

'It isn't, actually,' said Jollops gloomily. 'I've read all the books and not split me face once. There's nothing funny about comedy, believe me.'

'Why do it then?'

'Well, the pay's good. And there's a jester shortage. People are cryin' out for 'em, so I heard. Thought I might as well give it a go. If I pass the exam, I get a certificate. There's an award ceremony. I'll have to go up on stage an' tell an Original Joke. Then I gets presented with me Jester Jingling Stick and the three-pronged hat with the bells. Then it's goodbye servitude, hello show business.'

'Sounds exciting,' said Charlie encouragingly.

'Yeah.' Jollops gave a sigh. 'I'm havin' trouble with the Original Joke though. I've come up with one, but I'm not too sure about it.'

'Try it on me,' suggested Charlie. 'I like jokes.'

'You're sure?'

'Of course. Fire away.'

'Right then. Here goes.' Jollops cleared his throat rather self-consciously, then spoke in a high, squeaky voice, quite unlike his usual lugubrious mutter. 'Knock knock.'

'Er – who's there?'

'Jester,' squeaked Jollops.

'Jester who?' obliged Charlie.

'Jester minute, I've got no pants on.'

There was a little silence while Charlie digested this.

'Well, it's certainly original,' she managed, after a bit.

'Yeah. But is it funny?'

'Well – yes. Ish. Funnyish.'

'Really? I'm not sure about the pants. I mean, pants is a funny word. People laugh at pants. It's like sausages. But I'm thinkin', why would a jester be knocking on someone's door without his pants on? Unless he wanted to borrow a pair. But by sayin' "jester minute", it sounds like he's already got a pair of his own and is about to put them on, don't it? In which case, why didn't he put them on before he knocked at the door? See my problem?'

'It's only a joke, isn't it?' said Charlie. 'Why worry about the deeper meaning?'

'Mm. Maybe you're right. What did you think of the Comedy Voice?'

Some way behind, Dandypants nibbled on an apple and sulked. Much to his annoyance, Jollops and Charlie appeared to be getting on like a house on fire. He wondered what they were talking about.

He hoped it wasn't him.

That night, they dined on fish. Charlie had picked their campsite with care – a spot on higher ground so they could see any bears, wolves, witches or rampaging mobs approaching and defend themselves with greater ease. Jollops saw to Betsy, Dennis and Petal the pony, then gathered wood for a fire. Charlie set off for a nearby brook, armed with a small fishing rod that she had put together with a cut-off branch and a length of twine. Dandypants just sat around being useless. He was all set to scoff when she got back. He even ran through a few sneery put-downs in his head, along the lines of, *Oh dear. Rod not up to the job then?* Or *Big, was it? The one that got away?*

But he wisely kept his mouth closed when she arrived back a short while later with three fair-sized trout and a handful of wild parsley for garnishing. Was there nothing the girl couldn't do?

He had to admit that the trout was delicious. He was now lying on his back among scented pine needles, sucking his fingers and staring at the moon. Jollops was fast asleep and dreaming, by the sound of it. Every so often he would shout out strange sentences in a high, squeaky voice, then break into giggles or, occasionally, sobs. He had been acting oddly lately and seemed to have something on his mind. He wouldn't be parted from his sack and got very cagey when asked about the contents. Dandypants wondered what was in it.

Then he wondered if, even now, his clothes were on fire. What a depressing thought.

'Still mourning your clothes?' Charlie sat opposite him, her face glowing red in the firelight. 'There's no point, you know. They're gone. So what? Not all girls care as much about fancy clobber as you seem to think they do.'

'Don't they?' said Dandypants, surprised. 'I would have thought that'd be right at the top of the list. I mean, I know *you* don't care, that's obvious – ooops. Sorry. Slipped out.'

'That's OK. I know some people think I'm weird, dressing in breeches. They're more practical than a dress. I have *got* a dress, you know. I just don't wear it much.'

'Is that it?' said Dandypants, pointing to the floppy parcel lying on the ground next to her. He was dying to know what was in it. Charlie was as cagey about her parcel as Jollops was about his sack.

'No,' said Charlie shortly.

There was a little pause.

'So you think I'll make a good impression then?' said Dandypants hopefully. 'In spite of the mud and the holes and the hair and everything?'

'I only know about ordinary people. I haven't a clue about princesses. But if King Boris's daughter is halfway decent, she won't care twopence what you look like. Anyway, why do you care? You don't really want to get married, do you?'

'No,' admitted Dandypants. 'You know I don't. It's all the Masked Avenger's fault. I'd like to get my hands on him. What's he picking on me for? What have I ever done to him? Who is he anyway? Why is he hiding behind a mask? Why is he doing this? Does he really care about the peasants? What's in it for him? Why? Why? Why?'

'Search me,' said Charlie, with a shrug. 'I'm going to sleep. You take first watch. Wake me if there's trouble.'

'But I don't have a weapon. Can I borrow your sword?'

'No,' said Charlie firmly. 'Just wake me, OK?' And she rolled herself up in a blanket and began to snore.

Dandypants felt slightly miffed. He had wanted to talk long into the night about the meaning of it all, but it seemed that it wasn't to be.

She *had* tried to cheer him up though, in her weird sort of way.

Perhaps she wasn't so bad.

CHAPTER TWELVE

AND NOW TO **VULGARIA** (WHERE EVERYTHING'S BIGGER)

*Dandypants and Jollops gain admittance to the palace and
certain items are removed from the wash room.*

Vulgaria was a much bigger kingdom than Blott. King
Boris liked big things. He had a big palace and a big
army. He had a big wife and a big family of seven girls,
all of whom were married off, except the youngest, who
was proving difficult to shift.

King Boris's hobby was collecting countries. He was
the sort of person who liked a lot of room to expand.
Over the years, he had increased his territory by simply
marching into the smaller, surrounding countries of
Terrazaland, Begonia and Flog, giving the reigning
families the option of handing over the palace keys or
putting out to sea in a small, leaky boat. Then it was just
a question of flying the Vulgarian flag from the topmost
tower and holding a big celebration feast, where the
defeated monarch was expected to hand around the

cheese crackers. Another kingdom, another palace. Easy.

The only country that hadn't been swallowed up in this way was the small neighbouring country of Blott. This stuck in King Boris's gullet. Many years ago, as boys, King Boris and King Edward had gone to the same school, St Aloof's, whose motto was Play the Game. They had disliked each other intensely and ran with different crowds. Edward was tight and never shared the contents of his tuck box. Boris was loud and overbearing and good at conkers.

There was a certain Incident in the playground.

However, as much as one might like to, there was an unwritten rule about invading the countries of fellow Old Aloofees. It just wasn't considered good form. Apart from anything else, it made for a bad atmosphere at school reunions, which took place every year and which all old boys were expected to attend, no excuses, no exceptions. The terrifying nonagenarian known as The Old Headmaster *(shiver, shiver!)* presided over these occasions, and was very strict about such matters. So King Boris resisted the temptation of rushing in and conquering Blott in his usual, heavy-handed manner, although he was itching to do so.

King Boris's palace lay slap bang in the middle of Vulgaria's capital city, Glamorre. It was a city of tall towers and elegant houses. Smart coaches bowled along its bustling, cobbled streets. The citizens looked prosperous and reasonably cheerful. There was a school and a hospital. There were shops. There was a night watchman, decent drainage, a regular litter collection and working water pumps on every street corner. All the things that the disgruntled inhabitants of Skwaller could only dream about.

King Boris believed in keeping his subjects happy – not because he cared a fig about them, but because internal riots were such a *nuisance*. They distracted him from the real business of going out conquering new lands, which was what he enjoyed most. Besides, it was good for the ego to be greeted by cheering crowds throwing confetti and shouting *'Bless you, your majesty!'* whenever he drove through the streets resplendent in his golden coach.

Oh yes. Glamorre was a far cry from Skwaller.

'Well now!' said Jollops as they rode up the main street towards the palace gates. 'This is more like it. I think I'll move here.'

But Dandypants, impressed though he was with his first sight of foreign climes, had more pressing things on his mind. He had caught sight of himself in a shop window, and gone quite pale with shock.

'What am I going to *do*?' he fretted. 'I know you say appearances shouldn't matter, Charlie, but just look at me! I'm covered in dried mud with holes in my hose and *twigs* in my hair, for crying out loud! And I haven't even got a *comb*! I look like a *joke*.'

'Say you thought it was Red Nose Day,' suggested Jollops. He knew all about Red Nose Day. It was a big day on the jester's calendar.

'Or Hallowe'en,' said Charlie, with a giggle. She caught sight of Dandypants's face. 'Sorry.'

'I'd buy myself a new outfit, but I've only got half a crown. That won't even buy a new pair of hose.'

'It's my half crown anyway,' Jollops reminded him.

'Perhaps they'll have a wash room,' said Charlie. 'You can have a bit of a wash and brush up.'

'I need more than a wash,' insisted Dandypants. 'I'm a prince, for goodness' sake. I've got standards to keep up.'

'Perhaps she'll go for your personality,' said Jollops, without much conviction.

'Do you really think so?'

'No.'

'Well, whatever you're going to do, I'd do it now,' said Charlie. 'Those guards are looking at you in a funny way.'

She was right. The guards standing outside the palace gates were eyeing them up and down with more than a little interest. There was a big one and a little one. The little one muttered something into the big one's ear and they both stared hard at Dandypants.

Just then, a smart scarlet coach came bowling up the street at a fast lick. It had plumes wherever plumes could possibly be placed, and was pulled by two snorting coal-black horses. It screeched to a halt at the palace gates.

'Prince Florentine of Flush, come to claim the hand of the princess,' came a high, whinnying voice from the interior. 'Hurry up there and let me pass.'

The guards saluted and ran to open the gates. The coach sped through, spraying gravel.

'Looks like you've got competition,' said Charlie. 'I'd get in there quick if I was you.'

'You're right,' said Dandypants. 'I suppose I'd better.' He felt a sudden pang of anxiety. The thought hadn't crossed his mind that there might be rival suitors for the princess's hand. He was about to wheel Betsy round, when a thought crossed his mind. He looked over at Charlie. 'So – this is goodbye then?'

'Yep,' said Charlie. She picked up the reins. 'Here's where we part. Don't expect me to wish you luck, because I think you're nuts. See you, Jollops. Keep up the good work.'

They both watched as she rode off down the road.

'That's a pity,' said Jollops. 'I felt better when she was around. All them knives.'

'What did she mean by that?' asked Dandypants suspiciously.

'What?'

'*Keep up the good work.* What work is she referring to? As far as I can see, you never do a stroke.'

'Are you going to stand here arguing or what?' said Jollops. 'Because they're about to shut the gates.'

'Ah. Right. Come on then. Follow me. I'll handle

this. Believe it or not, I am capable of doing some things on my own.'

And with more confidence than he felt inside, Dandypants wheeled Betsy round and rode up to the guards, who were indeed in the process of closing the gates. They eyed him suspiciously.

'Yeah?' said the biggest one.

'Prince Daniel of Blott,' announced Dandypants, in what he hoped were ringing tones. 'Come to claim the hand of the princess.'

The guards exchanged doubtful glances.

'Are you sure?' said the big one.

'Look,' said Dandypants haughtily. 'I might not look at my best right now, but that's no fault of mine. I happen to have had a slight accident. Now, stand back and let me and my manservant pass.'

'See if he's on the list, corporal,' instructed the big guard. The small one took a piece of paper from his pocket and ran his eyes down it.

'What you say your name was again?'

'Daniel! Daniel of Blott! How many more times?'

'He's not on it,' said the small guard. 'You're not on it,' he told Dandypants.

'I don't believe this!' stormed Dandypants. 'Two full days and nights of facing peril in the forest and you won't let me in because my name doesn't appear on some stupid *list*? Out of my way this minute!'

'Not until we see some identification,' said the big one.

'*Identify* myself? When I've given you my royal word?' Dandypants was scandalized. 'Whatever is the world coming to? I'm Prince Daniel of Blott, son of King Edward and Queen Hilda, and you'd jolly well better believe it.'

'You might just be saying that,' said the smaller guard. 'For all we know, you're Dirty Dick Dirt of Dirt House, Dirt Lane, Dirtsville. That's who you look like.'

'So show us some ID, pal, unless you want to feel the sharp end of my pike,' said the big one.

The atmosphere was getting rather tense. A small crowd of interested bystanders was beginning to gather. People were beginning to point.

'Problems, sergeant?' said a voice. A tall, rather lordly looking man dressed in purple-velvet robes with a matching plumed hat was standing in the gap between the almost-closed gates. He was dark haired and clean shaven. His eyebrows were raised in polite enquiry.

'This bloke 'ere says he's come for the princess's hand, sir,' explained the big guard, nodding his head at Dandypants.

'Sarge 'ere was just askin' for some I.D.,' added the small guard.

'Look,' ground out Dandypants, between clenched teeth. 'I am Prince Daniel of Blott! I've had a slight mishap in the forest, that's all. I keep telling them that, but …'

'Ah,' interrupted the tall man, with a silky smile. He swept off his hat and gave a low bow. 'Of course. Your highness, please accept my apologies. This is all an unfortunate misunderstanding. Thank you, sergeant, I'll take over from here. Corporal, open the gates for the prince.'

'At last!' cried Dandypants, greatly relieved. 'A man with sense! And you are …?'

'Lord Lushing, equerry to his Majesty the King. I take it you are here for the interview?'

'If you mean I'm here to claim the princess's hand in marriage, yes, I jolly well am.'

'Then allow me to conduct you to the waiting room, sire. You may leave your mounts at the gate. The stables are getting rather crowded. We have a full house this morning.'

'Right. Thanks. Erm – I don't suppose there's a chance of sprucing myself up? I'm rather travel-stained, I fear. Bit of a confrontation in the forest.'

'How very unfortunate. Of course, you are most welcome to use the palace facilities. Take your time. There are several suitors to be seen before you.'

'Really?' said Dandypants, with a frown. 'How many?'

'Six, I believe.'

'*Six?*'

'Oh, yes. Yesterday, there were eleven. There has been an extremely good response to the advertisement, your highness. You are by no means the only applicant. No decision will be made, of course, until all the suitors have been seen. Now, if you'll just follow me.'

And he turned on his heel and strode off up the driveway with Dandypants and Jollops hurrying in his wake.

'Wooo! Chandeliers in the bog. Posh,' said Jollops, looking around approvingly.

Indeed, the palace facilities were very grand. The white tiled floor had a fluffy pink rug placed just so. The washbasins had big, ornate, golden taps. The cubicle doors had golden knobs on. There were huge mirrors on the walls and mountains of king-sized, snowy-white towels. There were large bottles of complementary aftershave. The bars of soap had crowns stamped on them.

From behind one of the cubicle doors came splashing noises, and the sound of a whinnying voice raised in song. Outside the door, hanging from a hook, was a scarlet doublet and matching hose, together with a plumed hat and short cloak. A pair of shoes with silver buckles were neatly placed beneath, next to a sword encased in a scarlet sheath.

'Prince Florentine of Flush,' explained Lord Lushing, with a dry little smile. 'Availing himself of the shower facility. Now, if you will excuse me, I must be about my duties. When you are ready, turn right, walk along to the end of the corridor and up the flight of stairs. The throne room is at the end of the passageway. Big double doors with a crown on, you can't miss it. There is a waiting area outside. Tell the receptionist I sent you. And may I take this opportunity of wishing your royal highness the very best of luck.'

And he clicked his heels together, bowed, and departed, leaving Dandypants to stare at himself despondently in the huge mirror and Jollops to wander around stealing the soap and spraying himself with free aftershave.

'*I'm here to marry the princess, the princess, the princess …*' trilled Prince Florentine, splashing away, oblivious to the fact that he had company.

'Oh dear,' fretted Dandypants. 'A comb, a comb, my kingdom for a comb! Just look at me, Jollops. I'm a *wreck*. I don't know where to *start*. I'll never get the mud out of these clothes. They're simply beyond the pale. *Bother* those peasants. When I think of all those carefully selected outfits. And here I am, desperate to look my best, and I haven't a thing to wear.'

'Oh yes you have then,' said Jollops.

He put a finger to his lips, then pointed meaningfully at the hook from which the unseen warbler's clothes were suspended in all their dazzling red glory.

'No!' said Dandypants, shocked. 'We can't.'

'*I'm here to marry the princess, all on a summer day …*'

'Yes we can. Go on, put them on quick, while he's busy.'

'But he won't stay in there for ever. He'll come out and find his clothes gone and raise the alarm.'

'Not if we lock him in. Look, there's a key in the lock.'

'Fa-la, she'll fall in love with me, in love with me, in love with me ...'

'But what if he shouts? Someone will hear him.'

'I'll stand outside and keep guard. If he makes a racket, I'll sing or somethin'. How long does it take to propose? You'll be in and out in no time.'

'How do you make that out? You heard his lordship. There are six before me.'

'So see if someone'll swap. Failin' that, create a diversion and nip in while their backs are turned. Easy. Go on, nick his clothes. Now's your chance.'

'And we will live so happily, so happily, so happily ...'

'No. It's too mean. I'm a prince, Jollops. Princes have principles. Besides, his shoes are too small. I'll have to keep my green boots on, and red and green are not a happy combination. I don't like the cut of the doublet, either. And that cloak's *very* last year.'

'They're clothes, they're clean, they'll do. Go on. Just try on the hat.'

So Dandypants tried on the hat.

CHAPTER THIRTEEN

SIZING UP THE COMPETITION

*In which Dandypants makes the acquaintance of one
unfriendly receptionist and five rival suitors.*

'Yes?' said the thin-lipped woman behind the reception
desk.

'Prince Daniel of Blott,' said Dandypants. 'Come to
claim the hand of the princess.'

He wasn't very comfortable in the stolen clothes.
Scarlet wasn't one of his favourite colours. The doublet
was cut strangely and the hose were uncomfortably short
in the leg. The plumed hat was too big as well and kept
falling over his eyes. It was, however, a distinct
improvement on the mud-spattered rags that were
currently hanging on the golden hook outside the
shower cubicle, where Prince Florentine of Flush sang
blissfully on in a world of scented steam.

The receptionist pulled a sheet of paper towards her
and consulted it.

'You're not down here,' she said. 'I've got Florentine of Flush, Horace of Haze, Bunty of Kartoon, Butch of Dragonia, Kevin of Bland and Rufus of Ruffland. Definitely no Daniel of Blott.'

'I know. I haven't got an appointment. Lord Lushing said it would be all right.'

'Hmm. Well, Prince Florentine hasn't showed up yet. I suppose I can fit you in, as an extra. But you really should have made an appointment, you know. Take a seat.'

Dandypants looked around. Before him was a short passageway leading to a large set of double doors bearing a crown motif. The throne room, of course. To the side was a waiting area containing the receptionist's desk and five large sofas. Sitting slap bang in the middle of each was a rival suitor. Five arrogant, unfriendly faces glared at him, daring him to sit down. There was a small, unoccupied bench over by the window. He chose that.

He sat down carefully, trying not to bend his knees on account of the too-short hose. There was a pile of magazines on the window sill. He picked up a back issue of *Monarch!* and pretended to flip through the pages, while surreptitiously studying the competition.

Five of them, all sitting in stony silence, staring down their noses and trying to out-sneer each other. A short, fat one, dressed in a particularly foul shade of violet. A tall, skinny, languid one with a monocle. A tiny, rat-like one, with his hair parted in the middle. A big, muscular one in thigh boots, who was playing with his dagger. One with ginger hair, inadvisably dressed in a pink kilt. None was remotely handsome. In fact, all would have been strong contenders for the Worst Prince in the Universe title. No Charmings here, that was for sure. Dandypants relaxed a little. As long as Prince Florentine remained banged up, he was certainly in with a chance.

Restlessly, he turned and peered out of the window. It overlooked the stables where a clutch of splendid-looking coaches were parked. A group of coachmen stood around, idly chatting and drinking strong tea while they awaited the return of their royal masters. There was no sign of Betsy and Dennis. He hoped somebody was looking after them.

He wondered whether Prince Florentine had finished his ablutions yet. Even now, he might be hammering on the door, howling for his clothes. Jollops couldn't stand outside the door singing for ever, somebody was bound to suspect something.

'Erm — excuse me,' said Dandypants to the receptionist. His voice echoed in the silence. Ten eyes bored into him. 'How long will I have to wait, do you think?'

'I really have no idea,' said the receptionist stiffly.

'It's just that I'm in a bit of a hurry. I was just wondering whether any of these gentlemen would mind if I went first?'

'*Ai* certainly would!' That was the tall, haughty one with the monocle. 'Ai'll have you know, sir, ai've been sitting here since eleven o'clock. Mai appointment, sir, was for naine.'

'And you are?' enquired Dandypants.

'Prince Horace of Haze, sir.'

'Well, thanks for nothing, Horace. Remind me to jolly well not help *you* out the next time you need a favour.'

'Well, *really*!' Prince Horace bridled. 'Of all the confounded *impudence,* sir! I've a good mind to call you out in a *duel,* sir!'

'We've all got proper appointments,' spoke up the short, fat, violet one. (Bunty?) 'You're just an extra. Why should you get special treatment?'

'That's right!' chimed in the one in the thigh boots. (Butch?) 'We've all been waiting hours. I'm supposed to be playing polo right now. Who do you think you are, coming in here, trying to take somebody's else's turn?'

The little ratty one and the ginger one said nothing, but their unhelpful expressions made it very clear that, when it came to the question of appointments, flexibility did *not* enter the equation.

Just then, the huge double doors opened and a liveried flunky stepped out. He scurried to the reception desk and proceeded to mutter to the receptionist, who once again consulted her list.

'Good gracious!' cried Dandypants, suddenly leaping to his feet. He pointed through the window with a quavering finger. 'Whose coach is that? I do believe someone is making off with it!'

As a diversion, it stank, but it was the best he could think of. Rather to his surprise, it worked. Five outraged figures leaped to their feet and surged towards the window with cries of alarm.

'What?'

'What's going on?'

'Is it *main*? Oh, *surely* not!'

'Out of the way, man, let me see!'

And while they struggled and pushed and tripped over each other's swords in an effort to look out of the window, Dandypants ran for it. He ran past the startled flunkey and receptionist, up the short passage towards the double doors.

Easy.

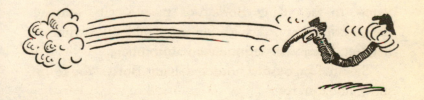

CHAPTER FOURTEEN

THE INTERVIEW

*In which our hero is goaded into biting off
more than he can chew.*

King Boris was fat. There is just no other way of putting
it. He sort of dripped over his throne, which was a big,
golden affair, studded with gigantic rubies. His daughter,
Princess Langoustina, sat next to him on a slightly
smaller version. Behind and to one side stood a footman
in a powdered wig, holding a tray containing a pile of
coloured scrolls.

Neither the king nor his beautiful daughter looked
happy. In fact, King Boris was purple with temper.
Langoustina slumped, with her arms folded, scowling at
her feet. There was definitely an atmosphere.

'Sit up, Langoustina,' ordered King Boris. 'You're on
show. Look pretty.'

'No,' pouted Langoustina. 'Why should I?'

King Boris gripped the arms of his throne with white

knuckles. You could almost see smoke coming from his ears.

'Are you defying me, young lady? I promised your mother I would have you engaged by the time she got back from your sister's. Who's going to marry you with a face like that?'

'I'm not getting married. I'm getting a salon. I'm going to be a hairdresser.'

'You'll do no such thing. You'll get married in a proper manner. Sit up. Smile.'

'No.'

King Boris could have screamed. He tried another tack.

'Langoustina,' he said. 'Remember those pretty glass slippers you wanted Daddy to buy you? They're yours. If you behave yourself.'

Just at that point, the first of the day's suitors came unexpectedly bounding through the doors. He was dressed from top to toe in dazzling scarlet. His flushed face had a hunted expression. There seemed to be something a little strange with his hose.

'A red one,' muttered Langoustina, making a face. 'Yuck.'

King Boris, with a huge effort, forced his lips into a regal smile of welcome.

'Ah,' he boomed. 'Today's first applicant, I take it. Good, good. Name?'

'Prince Daniel of Blott,' gasped Dandypants, with what he hoped was a winning smile. 'Come to claim the hand of the beautiful princess!'

'Hah!' muttered Langoustina. 'Dream on.'

'Daniel of Blott, eh?' King Boris's bushy eyebrows shot up to the rim of his crown. His fat fingers drummed on the arms of his throne. 'Well, well. This *is* unexpected.'

'Absolutely!' agreed Dandypants. 'I'm an unexpected, spontaneous, devil-may-care sort of guy, I am!' He snapped his fingers and slapped his thigh, his eyes flickering to Princess Langoustina to see what kind of effect he was having.

So this was his future bride! She had lots of tumbling yellow hair, big blue eyes and a rosebud mouth. All quite promising, if it wasn't for the fact that she was staring at him with the sort of expression normally reserved for a snail in a side salad.

Just then, the receptionist's head poked around the door. From somewhere behind her, came the sound of squawking voices raised in shrill protest.

'Excuse me, your Majesty,' she said grimly. 'There's something I think you should know. *This* young *gentleman* has taken it upon himself to ...'

'Yes, yes. Thank you, Miss Trimble, that will be all,' said King Boris, still drumming his fingers. He was staring hard at Dandypants with a strange expression.

'But ...'

'That'll be *all*, Miss Trimble. Go and do some filing.' He turned to Dandypants. 'You may approach the throne, young man.'

Dandypants treated the departing Miss Trimble to a brief, triumphant smirk, then strode towards the dais, snatched off Prince Florentine's hat and sank into a low bow, hoping that his hose would stand it. He wondered whether he should kiss the princess's hand, but noticed that she was keeping both hands firmly tucked into her armpits. Perhaps he wouldn't bother.

'All right, all right, that'll do,' said King Boris testily. 'Get up.'

Carefully, Dandypants did so. Much more of this, and his hose would be around his knees.

King Boris thrust his large face forward, brows bristling and small, beady eyes glittering.

'So, young man!' he barked. 'I take it you are the son of Edward of Blott? Or Old Teddy Tightwad, as he was affectionately known in the lower sixth. Am I right?'

'I am indeed, sire. Pops sends you his regards. He always speaks of you with great fondness.'

This was a lie, of course. But it was all in a good cause.

'Does he now?' rumbled King Boris. 'Just grateful that I don't invade his tin pot little country, more like. I could do it, you know. I could march in and take over Blott any time I like. It's only respect for the old school tie that holds me back, and he knows it.'

Next to him, Princess Langoustina gave a huge yawn.

'I'm bored,' she announced. 'Bored, bored, bored, bored, bored, bored, bored, *bored*. Are you going to talk about boring things all day?'

'Just a minute, Langoustina. Daddy's talking. So, tell me, Prince Dandypants.' The king looked fierce. 'Did your father put you up to this? Are you here in some sort of *spying* capacity? Or is it Langoustina's dowry Old Tightwad's after?'

'Certainly not!' said Dandypants, stung. 'This was my own idea. I saw the advertisement for your daughter's hand and decided to answer it, that's all. There was nothing about the sons of old school chums not being able to apply. Are you saying I'm not eligible?'

'I'm not saying anything yet. I'm still not sure about your motives for being here, young man. So tell me, Prince Daniel, how are things back home in little Blott? Things chugging along, are they? Any – *problems* at all?'

'Oh, no, no, everything's fine. Apart from the business with the peasants, everything's just …'

'Business with the peasants?' interrupted King Boris. 'What sort of business with the peasants?'

'Well, there's some chap calling himself the Masked Avenger who's trying to stir up trouble. There's talk of an uprising. As a matter of fact, I ran into a bit of bother myself. Booing, mud chucking, that sort of thing. And the night before last, a rampaging mob confronted me in the forest and stole my clothes. I tried to fight them off single-handed, but I was vastly outnumbered.'

Princess Langoustina gave a small, rude snort.

'Stole your *clothes*?' enquired the king curiously.

'Yes. You don't think I'd *choose* to wear red, do you? I am in … borrowed apparel.'

'Well, well! Robbed of your clothes, eh? You *have* had a rough ride. Tut tut, deary me. Whatever will these peasants think of next?'

Princess Langoustina could take no more. She stamped her foot.

'*Honestly!* I thought this was supposed to be all about *me,* Daddy! Is he going to ask for my hand in marriage or what?'

'I thought I did,' said Dandypants. 'When I came in.'

'No you didn't,' said Langoustina, with a snooty glare. 'Claiming's not the same as asking for, is it?'

'Oh. Well – can I have it then? Your hand?'

'No,' said Princess Langoustina triumphantly.

'Langoustina!' thundered King Boris. 'If you don't stop humiliating your suitors and sit up and look pretty I will be *very cross* with you! Remember the shoes?'

'All right, all right, keep your crown on. But I'm not sitting here all morning, I want to wash my hair. Give him the challenge and let's move on to the next one.'

Dandypants's ears pricked up. Challenge? What was this?

Puzzled, he watched as King Boris clicked his fingers at the waiting footman, who came forward bearing the tray of coloured scrolls.

'Go on,' said King Boris. 'Which colour?'

'What do you mean?' said Dandypants, puzzled.
'What's all this about?'

'The interview's over. Now it's Heroic Deed Time.
Choose your Challenge. Each scroll has a different quest
with varying degrees of danger. Pink's easy, yellow's no
picnic, blue's tricky, orange is hard, red's confoundedly

difficult and purple's well nigh impossible. You get extra points if you choose a purple one.'

'Quest?' said Dandypants. 'The advert didn't say anything about going on a quest.'

'Good gracious, young man!' rumbled King Boris. 'You didn't think you could just walk in here and claim my daughter's hand without some sort of traditional challenge, surely?'

'Well – yes, as a matter of fact.'

'Then think again. You're not the only one in the running. I'll have you know there's a lot of competition for Langoustina's hand. There has to be a proper weeding out process. She'll choose the suitor who proves himself the most worthy.' Langoustina opened her mouth. 'Or she will if she wants those shoes,' added the king. Langoustina closed it again.

'Well, this is a bit much,' said Dandypants rather huffily. 'I do think you should have made it clear in the advert. I thought it would be straightforward. Come along, pop the question, get engaged, wedding bells ring, bob's your uncle. And now, all of a sudden, after all the trouble I had getting here, I'm to go off on some sort of *quest*.'

'Don't bother,' said Langoustina nastily. 'You wouldn't succeed anyway.'

'I might,' said Dandypants, annoyed.

'No you wouldn't. You don't look a bit heroic to me. I bet *bunny rabbits* frighten you.'

'No they don't. I happen to know a rabbit very well. His name is Stuart. I handle him often. And quests are easy. I've been on loads.'

'I don't believe you. Why, I bet *you'd* even fail the *pink* one. Pink's so easy a baby could do it. Not *you* though.'

'Now, now, Langoustina,' chided the king, who had been listening to this exchange with interest. 'Don't force the lad into making a fool of himself. Old Tightwad was always thought of as a bit of a mummy's boy. Like father, like son. Not everyone can be a hero.'

Dandypants drew himself up to his full height. Something around the waist area of the stolen hose went ping, but he ignored it. His eyes flickered over the tray of scrolls.

'Which is the well nigh impossible?' he enquired stiffly.

'Purple,' chorused King Boris and Langoustina.

With a tight little smile, Dandypants reached out and took a purple one. Foolhardy, he knew — but there were times in a chap's life when he had to jolly well make a stand.

'There,' he said, with a tight little sneer. 'That surprised you, didn't it? Now you see what kind of fellow you're dealing with. Call me a mad, crazy fool if you like! Well, I am! I laugh in the face of danger, I do! I'm going now. I suppose you think that's the last you'll see of me. But you're wrong! I shall return!'

And with that, he slapped his thigh, turned on his heel and stalked from the room, hoping that his hose wouldn't fall down.

'Dad,' said Langoustina. 'If you expect me to marry *that* ...'

'Langoustina,' interrupted the king. 'Go and wash your hair or do some spinning or something.'

'But I thought there were lots more suitors to see.'

'Later. Daddy has some business to attend to. Hair. Wash it. Now.'

Ten minutes later, when Langoustina had flounced out, the king was talking urgently to Lord Lushing.

Instructions were issued.

A large bag of gold changed hands.

CHAPTER FIFTEEN

*In which Charlie delivers a certain tapestry to Lady Lushing,
who really should get out more.*

Meanwhile …

'Yes?' said Lady Lushing, peering through her
monocle. She stood at the castle door – a short, plump,
fluffy, excitable little woman with piled up orange hair.
Right now, she seemed a little harassed.

'Special delivery,' said Charlie, holding up the parcel.

'The tradesman's entrance is round the back. Didn't
you see the notice on the gate? Delivery boys to the
back, it says.'

'Ah, but you see, I'm a delivery *girl*. Don't apologize,
everyone makes the same mistake. I'm Willard
Tuffgrissel's niece. I've brought the tapestry.'

'Oh! *Right*. I see!' Lady Lushing clapped her hands
together and squealed with excitement. 'Do *forgive* me,
Miss Tuffgrissel. I've got the builders in, I wasn't

thinking. I'm an *enormous* admirer of your uncle's work. So very good of him to fit me in at such short notice. Come in, come in. Mind the buckets.'

She turned and trotted into the castle, with Charlie following behind.

'You'll have to excuse the mess,' said her ladyship. 'I'm having the castle *completely* refurbished from top to bottom!'

'So I see,' said Charlie, staring around at the Great Hall. Everywhere she looked, there were men on ladders with buckets of paint. More men were traipsing to and fro carrying oil paintings, pieces of antique furniture, assorted ancient weapons and suits of armour. The rugs had been rolled back from the flagstones and were stacked in a corner.

'I'm going for a *totally* new look,' explained Lady Lushing, gesturing with her monocle. 'I've had a lot of time on my hands recently and, quite frankly, the décor's been getting to me. All that doomy antique stuff, so old hat, don't you think? So I decided to have a clean sweep. I'm getting rid of all the old rubbish that's been in my husband's family for generations and replacing the lot!'

'Wow,' said Charlie. 'Does he know?'

'No! That's the thing!' Lady Lushing gave a little trill of laughter. 'It'll be a lovely, *lovely* surprise! I'm covering up those chilly old stone walls with rose-pink wallpaper. Pale-blue rafters, I thought. A new three-piece suite, of course, instead of those ghastly old horse-hair armchairs he claims to like so much. And lace curtains, to hide the draughty old windows. Brand-new peach-coloured fitted carpets throughout. And lots of pictures of fluffy little animals and flowers to brighten the place up. I can't wait to see his face.'

'Mmm,' said Charlie. 'I'm sure it'll be worth seeing.'

'Won't it! He doesn't suspect a thing, of course! He's been away a lot recently.'

'Really?'

'Oh, yes. In fact, he's at the palace now. On *Royal Business.*' Her ladyship looked sideways at Charlie to see if this had the desired effect. 'He's the king's equerry, you know. He's very pally with King Boris. *Very* pally.'

'Is that a fact?' Charlie suppressed a yawn. 'Well, well. Pally, eh?'

'Oh yes. I see that impresses you. And so it should.

I'd go so far as to say that my husband is King Boris's right-hand man. Well, of course, the king needs someone he can trust. He's rather tied up at the moment, trying to get his daughter married off. She's proving rather obstinate, apparently. But listen to me, chattering on! You'll be wanting to start work. Hanging the tapestry is part of the service, I take it?'

'Yep,' said Charlie, hefting the large parcel. 'I'll stick it up for you. Where do you want it?'

'In his lordship's study. That's where he spends most of his time. On the rare occasions when he's home.' Lady Lushing's eyes narrowed for a moment and her mouth went rather tight. Then she recovered her good humour

and smiled at Charlie. 'Won't it be lovely for him? Instead of all those doomy old portraits of his ancestors, he'll be able to feast his eyes on darling little puppies frolicking in a rose garden. Follow me, Miss Tuffgrissel.'

Excitedly, she scurried off down a long, stone corridor where several glum men in cloth caps were busily slapping paste on to lengths of flowery wallpaper. Charlie followed, picking her way between trestle tables, ladders and buckets of paste.

'Here!' said Lady Lushing, throwing open a door. 'In you come.'

The study was a gloomy room with high ceilings. Three of the four walls were lined with serious-looking books. The fourth wall consisted of oak panelling. Stern, unpleasant faces stared forth from dark oil paintings that had probably hung there undisturbed for hundreds of years. A large, polished desk was placed beneath the small window which looked out on to the tidy lawn.

'Horrid, isn't it?' said Lady Lushing cheerily. 'So dark and depressing. But nothing that a pair of pretty curtains and a coat of pink paint can't put right. And the tapestry, of course. You can spread it out on the floor. Oh, I simply can't wait to see it! A genuine Tuffgrissel. My friends will be green with envy.'

Charlie took out one of her knives and sliced through the string. She tore off the wrapping paper and shook out the carefully folded tapestry, then spread it on the polished boards.

It wasn't one of Uncle Willard's best works, she reflected. Frolicking puppies in rose gardens weren't really up his street. But if the customer wanted puppies and roses, puppies and roses is what the customer got. At any rate, Lady Lushing seemed thrilled.

'Perfect!' she gasped, peering through her monocle. 'So lifelike! Look at the adorable little black and white one with the butterfly on his nose! And the darling little brown one with the melting eyes, chasing his tail. Miss Tuffgrissel, your uncle is a genius!'

'Where did you say you want it hung?' asked Charlie.

'On the wall facing the desk. It'll cover up that horrid brown wood.'

'But it's polished oak panelling! Sixteenth century, by the looks of it. I'm not sure I should be hammering nails into it.'

'Oh, pooh! I've been dying to get rid of it for years. I'd have it ripped out, but I think the castle might fall down. Covering it up is the next best thing.'

'But what about the portraits?'

'Oh, take them down. Nasty old things, they're well past their sell-by date. Throw them in a pile, I'll get someone to remove them later. Do you have everything you require?'

'I've got a hammer and nails, yes, and a needle and thread, and hooks and a measuring tape. I'll need a thin length of wood which I'd like to cut myself. I have to sew the top edge to a supporting rod, you see, and then ...'

Just then, there came the sound of a distant crash, followed by raised voices. Lady Lushing winced.

'Oh dear, *now* what have they done? I daren't take my eyes off these workmen for a moment. Will you excuse me, Miss Tuffgrissel? I'll send along one of the carpenters with some samples of wood. There are plenty of ladders about, should you need them. Can you manage by yourself?'

'Yep,' said Charlie. 'Just leave me to it. I'll let you know when I've finished.'

Lady Lushing scuttled off, leaving Charlie to get on with it.

She stared around at the austere room. Through the window, she could see a team of men hurling rare antiques and priceless articles of furniture into a large cart, ready to be taken to the junk heap. His lordship would certainly get a surprise on his return. Somehow, she felt it wouldn't be a lovely one. But then, reflected Charlie, that was none of her concern. She had a job to do.

With a little sigh, she took out her tape measure and got to work.

CHAPTER SIXTEEN

THE QUEST

In which Dandypants and Jollops eat an overpriced
lunch and thrash out a plan.

'I don't think I heard you right,' said Jollops. 'We're goin'
on a what?'

'A quest!' snapped Dandypants irritably. 'A quest, a
quest! A purple one! A purple quest! How many more
times?'

'Nope. Still didn't get it. Run it past me again.'

They were sitting in Bad Bill's Bar – a dark, dingy,
deserted little inn situated down a cobbled side alley.
There were much nicer places to go in Glamorre, of
course, but Dandypants had opted for somewhere
obscure, in case Prince Florentine came looking for him.
Right now, they were tucked into a dark corner, waiting
for Bad Bill to serve them with some much-needed
lunch.

'You're being stupid on purpose, just to annoy me,

aren't you, Jollops? Look, I'll put it as simply as I can. I had to choose from a selection of coloured scrolls. Each is a different quest. It's a test of bravery.'

'The advert never said nothin' about no quest.'

'I know, I *know*. Don't you think I pointed that out? Anyway. The scrolls came in six colours. Pink, yellow, blue, orange, red and purple, in order of difficulty.'

'And you chose purple,' said Jollops, in hollow tones.

'Well, yes!'

'The hardest.'

'Yes! I was *goaded* into it, Jollops. I took it to prove a point. My honour was at stake. It's all very well for you. It was me who had to stand there, dressed like Mr Strawberry, getting the third degree from King Boris and having my bravery called into question by that beastly girl.'

'You mean your future bride. I take it you didn't like her much.'

'Loathed her, but that's beside the point. The point is, she *sneered* at me. I had to put up with a lot of rude sneering. All you had to do was hang about outside the bathroom, doing nothing.'

'Mmm,' said Jollops.

Actually, Jollops had spent quite an eventful half hour outside the bathroom. While Prince Florentine was still singing away in the shower, he had snatched the opportunity to catch up on his reading. He managed half a chapter of *So You Want to Be a Jester?* before his eyes started to close and he had to put it away. While Prince Florentine dried himself, he worked on his Original Joke. When Prince Florentine finally emerged from the cubicle and spotted that his clothes were missing, Jollops tried out a Comic Dance, which had the effect of drowning out the muffled wails and thumping noises coming from behind the locked door. Several passing maids and footmen had gathered to watch. He thought he was going down quite well – although he had to admit the audience looked more scared than amused. At any rate, after staring hard at him slapping his knees and kicking up his heels, they began to hurry away. Jollops had a feeling they were about to call the palace guards.

Prince Florentine was really getting into his stride now. He was attempting to break out of his prison with a towel rail he had wrenched from the wall. The door was beginning to splinter. Any minute now he'd be out and running around in his towel looking for his clothes, all pink, steaming outrage, and if he bumped into Dandypants there would be Serious Trouble.

Jollops, then, was more than relieved when Dandypants, looking grim but determined, came bounding down the corridor waving a rolled-up purple piece of paper. Together, without a word, they had fled the place, pausing only to collect Betsy and Dennis who were wandering unattended around the gardens helping themselves to lunch from the carefully tended flower beds.

'Double pie'n-mash-wiv-peas-two-large-jam-dough-nuts-wiv-side-ordera-soy-sauce-two-tankards-ale.' A large tray came crashing down on the table between them. Lunch had arrived. 'That'll be 'alf a crown,' said Bad Bill, holding out a hand like a ham.

'It's nine pence,' said Jollops, pointing to a large sign which said *All Yew Kin Scof fur Nin Pens*. 'Think we're stupid? You're havin' us on because we're not from round these parts.'

'Want a fight, shorty?' said Bad Bill. He had an attitude problem, which is why his bar was always deserted.

Dandypants paid him half a crown and he went away, looking a bit disappointed. For a while, there were no sounds apart from chewing and slurping noises. It had been a long time since their fish supper the night before.

'So what's it all about? This quest?' asked Jollops, when the worst hunger pangs had subsided.

'I don't know. I haven't had time to look at it, have I?'

'Well, now's as good a time as any. Go on. Ruin my day.'

'All right. I must admit, I'm curious.'

Dandypants fished around and produced the purple scroll. He undid the ribbon, broke the wax seal and unrolled it. His eyes moved along the lines. He went pale.

'Oh dear,' he said. 'Oh deary, deary me.'

'What?' said Jollops. 'What's the matter?'

'Well, put it this way. Maybe — just *maybe* I should have chosen pink.'

'It don't involve a dragon, do it? Because if it do, you can count me out,' said Jollops firmly. 'I can't abide dragons. It's me asthma.'

'No. No dragons. Er — how do you feel about giants?'

'I'm a dwarf. How do you think I feel? Why?'

'Listen to this. *Your task is as follows. You are to take the road out of Glamorre. Follow it for two leagues until you come to a signpost pointing to The Big House. The house belongs to a giant. His name is Gorgonzola. Your task is to bring back three hairs from his head.*'

'That's it?'

'That's it.'

'It's a stinker,' said Jollops.

'Isn't it?' groaned Dandypants. 'Apart from anything else, it's totally pointless. I could understand if I had to bring back something useful, like a golden-egg-laying hen or a magic harp or … or … or seven league boots, or … or … or …'

'Gold,' supplied Jollops.

'Exactly! But risking one's life for *three gigantic hairs*. Totally, utterly mindless. What will they do with them? Frame them, or flush them away, or what?'

'They're taking the mick,' agreed Jollops. 'Tell you what. Don't let's bother. Let's just ride on. There must be other princesses you can try.'

'Oh, I can't do that! It's personal now. If you'd seen the smirks on their faces, you'd understand. I'll show them what kind of guy they're dealing with. I'm jolly well going to get those hairs if it's the last thing I do.'

'It will be,' said Jollops. 'You don't mess with giants. What's his name again?'

'Gorgonzola.'

'There you go. Name like that, he's sure to be a big cheese. Crunch your bones as soon as look at you, I shouldn't wonder. What are you plannin' to do? Sneak into his bedroom and give him a short back and sides while he sleeps? Rather you than me.'

'Don't be silly, Jollops. That way is fraught with peril. He'd be sure to wake up. Far too risky.'

'What, then? Challenge him to a duel? *Give me those hairs, fatty, or it'll be the worse for you* sort of thing?'

'Well, of course, that'd *look* good …'

'But it would be stupid,' added Jollops.

'Yes,' conceded Dandypants rather wistfully. 'Yes, I suppose it would. Willard Tuffgrissel did warn me not to rely on my fencing skills.'

'It's a shame we haven't got Charlie,' said Jollops. 'She could do it.'

'Well, we don't,' said Dandypants. 'So fighting's out. No, a bit of clever trickery is called for here. Come on, man, think. It can't be *that* difficult.'

'We can dress up as strolling hairdressers.'

'Don't be ridiculous. At the very least we'd need a comb. Thanks to you, we don't even have *that*. And then there's scissors and shampoo and stuff and we don't have any money. That was our last half crown.'

'*My* last half crown.'

'Oh, stop being so petty-minded. *Think*. There must be hundred of ways of parting people from their hair.'

'We can walk up to his front door and say we're collectin' hairs for the Baldy Society and ask him for a contribution,' suggested Jollops. He was good at sarcasm. He was surprised it wasn't part of the jesters' course.

There was a short silence. Then:

'Do you know, Jollops,' said Dandypants slowly. 'Do you know, I think you might have something there. It's certainly novel. And so simple, it just might work. I mean, giants aren't known for their brains, are they? Rumour has it they're pretty stupid. And it would save an awful lot of unnecessary danger and unpleasantness. Yes, the more I think about it, the more I like it. You'll need a tin, of course.'

'*I'll* need a tin?'

'Well, yes. You'll do the asking and I'll be there hiding with my sword – well, Florentine's sword – ready to back you up if necessary. But it won't be. Nobody assaults charity workers, do they?'

'Why me? Why can't you do the askin'?'

'For two reasons. Firstly, you look the part. I mean, even in Florentine's clothes and with these tights, anyone can tell I'm a dashing prince, can't they? I'd hardly be collecting door to door for charity.'

'That's one reason. What's the second?'

'I order you to. Who's boss around here anyway?'

'Yeah, yeah, all right,' sighed Jollops. 'I'll do it. You'd only muck it up anyway.'

'Good. Come on. We'll need to get cracking if you're going to pinch a tin before the shops close.'

'*I'm* gonna pinch a tin …?'

CHAPTER SEVENTEEN

THE GIANT

GORGONZOLA

*In which Dandypants and Jollops put
their plan into operation.*

The Big House, home sweet home to the giant
Gorgonzola, was situated in the countryside, well away
from Glamorre. King Boris was quite happy to have a
resident giant living in his kingdom – in fact, it came in
rather useful from time to time – but not on his own
doorstep, thanks very much. Giants weren't popular in
urban areas. They cracked pavements, caused horse pile-
ups and scared little children. So, in time-honoured
fashion, Gorgonzola lived on a hill all by himself in a
massive, ivy-covered, ramshackle house, surrounded by
the traditional overgrown, weed-ridden garden.

Dandypants and Jollops peered furtively through the
rusty bars of the large, sagging gate, which hung on one
hinge. A lopsided notice was attached with string. The
words *Privit! Keep Owt!* were written on it in black chalk.

'It's in a bit of a state, isn't it?' said Dandypants. 'He might be a giant, but he's not big on house work. Look at the state of the garden. And all the windows are cracked, look.'

'I don't like it,' said Jollops. 'Creepy. Brrr.'

'Have you ever seen a giant in the flesh, Jollops?' Dandypants was craning his neck to see through the rusty bars. The weed-ridden path led up to a tall, off-putting front door, which was painted black and had an iron knocker. Right now, it was firmly closed.

'Nope. There was one lived over by Puddling in my granny's day.'

'Really? What became of him? Did some heroic type run him through with his sword?'

'Moved, I think. Got fed up with paying taxes to your dad.'

'Oh. Right.'

'I seen pictures of 'em though. Terrifyin'. Tall as a mountain. Two headed, some of 'em. An hairy. Horribly hairy shoulders reachin' up to the stars. An they've all got great big …'

'All right, all right, that'll do. Stop trying to put me off. Besides, you're thinking of ogres. He can't be *that* big, can he? He'd never fit in the house. Anyway, that's enough peering. Go over your lines once more.'

'What, *again*?'

'*Yes* again. You have to be word-perfect. Look innocent, and be polite. Remember, I'll be right beside you in case you need back-up. Have you got the tin?'

'Yep,' said Jollops, producing a tin which until an hour or so ago had held pineapples. It now contained hairs, cut from the tails of Betsy, and Dennis, who both had plenty and couldn't care less about losing a few for a good cause. The tin was now denuded of its label and had the letters WFTB scratched on the side.

'Good. And your official badge?'

Jollops had a badge too, bearing the same initials. They had made it from a beer mat borrowed from Bad Bill's Bar and attached it to Jollops's tunic with a bent nail they had found in the road. Jollops pointed to it wordlessly.

'Right. Once again then. From the top.'

Gorgonzola sat watching them from behind a ragged curtain, his yellow teeth bared in a huge smile of anticipation. He was so excited, he could barely contain himself. He had been sitting in his bedroom, snacking on walnuts, out of his mind with boredom and staring out of the window when he had first seen them come riding up the hill. There was a red one and a small brown one. Two! It had been a long time since Gorgonzola had had any visitors – or victims, as he liked to call them – and now, all of a sudden, there were two!

Gorgonzola chortled to himself and cracked his large knuckles. He wondered whether the king had sent them. He hoped so. There would be money in it if the king was involved. Of course, they might have come off their own bat, for whatever reason, which wouldn't be *quite* so good. But either way, things were looking up. It had been a long time since Gorgonzola had had any slaves. There was an *awful* lot of washing up to do.

He watched them tether their mounts to a tree and peer in through the gate. After a bit of talk, the red one

drew his sword, squeezed through the bars and ducked behind some undergrowth. Gorgonzola watched him circle around the bushes, obviously taking care not to be seen. He ended up behind a tree growing close to the front door. He then beckoned urgently to the little brown one, who came trudging up the path holding what looked like a tin in his hand. Hmm. Interesting.

Gorgonzola let the curtain drop and sat back, waiting.

It was all Jollops could do to reach the knocker. He stood on tiptoe, fingertips straining to grasp it.

'Come on!' hissed Dandypants from behind the tree.

'Can you reach it or can't you?'

'All right, all right, hang on, I'm tryin'... there. That's got it.'

Bang! The heavy knocker clanged against the door. Inside, echoes reverberated.

There was a long silence.

Then footsteps. Heavy, clumping footsteps. Drawing closer.

Jollops bit his lip and thought of his correspondence course. Think positive, that was the thing. Another month or two and he'd be jesting away for loads of money in some nice, safe, faraway kingdom and all this sort of thing would be behind him. He patted his sack of books for luck.

There came a rattle of chains and the sound of bolts being drawn back. Then the door opened and he found himself staring at a pair of vast knees. His eyes travelled up – past the studded belt, past the barrel chest enclosed in a worn leather jerkin, past the massive shoulders to the head. Thankfully, there was only one of those – but it wasn't pretty. A thundering great, grizzled moon of a face, framed by lank locks of greasy hair. Two vast ears stuck out on either side, adorned with brass hoops. Two watery, red-rimmed eyes stared down at him.

'YES?' boomed Gorgonzola. Except that it was more long and drawn out than that. It was more like: 'YEEEEEERRRRSSSSSS?'

Jollops swallowed hard. He was on.

'Sorry to bother you, sir,' he said brightly, in his squeaky comedy voice. 'I wonder if you can spare two minutes of your time?'

'I IS NOT WANTING DE DOUBLE GLAZIN'
OR DE PATIO DOORS.'

'Of course not. Who would? No, I'm collectin' for charity on behalf of WFTB. Wigs For The Bald, supporters of the follicley challenged, you may have heard of us. I am, as you can see, a registered collector. This is my official badge, and this 'ere is my trusty hair collectin' tin. And before you shut the door in my face, let me make it clear that I am *not* askin' for money.'

Gorgonzola stared stupidly at the tin. He frowned. He scratched his head. Then he stared at Jollops again.

'WHAT DIS? YOU IS WANTIN' MONEY?'

Jollops relaxed a bit. Yes, the rumours had been right. Giants *were* stupid.

'No money, sir,' he explained patiently. 'Hair. Spare hair. If everyone I called on stumped up three hairs, *just three hairs,* baldness would be eradicated and the world would be a happier place. You appear to have been blessed with an excellent crop, sir, if I might say so. Would you care to make a donation?'

Behind the tree, Dandypants couldn't believe his ears. Jollops always spoke in a lugubrious mutter. What was this new, jolly, stupidly squeaky voice all about? Could it be nerves?

Gorgonzola stared down from his great height. Then he smiled, displaying a row of jagged, picket-fence teeth. Then he bent down, stretched out a huge hand and patted Jollops on his head.

'YOU CUTE LITTLE FELLER,' he rumbled approvingly. 'GOT FUNNY, SQUEAKY VOICE.'

'Thanks very much,' squeaked Jollops.

'COME ON IN. ME MAKE YOU CUP OF TEA.'

'Very kind, but it's not necessary. Just give me the hairs and I'll be on my way.'

'AH, GO ON. JUST A QUICK ONE. ME NEVER GET VISITORS. ME GO AND PUT KETTLE ON.' He turned and looked hard at the tree behind which Dandypants was hiding. 'RED ONE COME IN TOO,' he added.

And with that, he turned and shambled off into the shadows.

Rather sheepishly, Dandypants emerged from behind the tree and joined Jollops on the doorstep.

'Funny that,' he said. 'I could have sworn I was well-concealed.'

'Now what?' said Jollops. 'Do we scarper or what?'

'I don't know,' said Dandypants. 'What do you think?'

'Goin' in for tea wasn't part of the plan.'

'True. But he seems harmless enough.'

They both peered uncertainly into the dark hall. From somewhere inside came the distant clink of tea cups.

'Could be a trap,' said Jollops.

'No,' said Dandypants. 'I don't think so. He's just a lonely old giant who wants a bit of company. I think we should play along with him. Go in, have a chat and a sociable cup of tea, get the hairs and be on our way. Come on. I'll do the talking from now on. I can't take much more of that squeaky voice you've suddenly adopted.'

Together they stepped into the dark hall.

CHAPTER EIGHTEEN

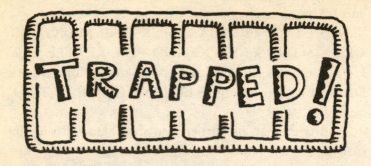

*In which Dandypants and Jollops venture into the Giant's
kitchen and discover that all is not as it seems.*

The kitchen was a slum. Dozens of greasy crocks and
pots filled the sink and draining board. More were piled
on the kitchen table. The huge, black kitchen range was
thick with grease. A big kettle sat on top, belching steam.
Three large mugs were set out on a filthy work surface,
together with a big, chipped, blue-and-white-striped
milk jug, a bowl of sugar and a massive ancient brown
teapot. There was also a giant-sized tin of chocolate
biscuits.

Gorgonzola was carefully spooning tea into the pot,
humming away to himself in a deep, chesty rumble. He
looked up as his visitors appeared in the doorway and
put on his best, welcoming smile.

'DERE YOU IS,' he said. 'TEA NEARLY READY.'

'Well, I must say, this is jolly good of you,' said

Dandypants. 'It's not often we get offered tea in our line of work, is it, Jollops?'

'NO?' enquired Gorgonzola, rummaging around in a cupboard. 'AH! GINGER CAKE! ME KNEW ME HAD SOME! YOU LIKE CAKE?'

'Well, yes. I must say a slice of cake would go down a treat.'

'WHY YOU STAND IN DOORWAY? ME SCARE YOU?'

'Oh, no, no, of course not! Perish the thought!' protested Dandypants. He nudged Jollops. Cautiously, they advanced into the kitchen. High over their heads, the rafters were hung with great bunches of onions and garlic. There was washing hanging up there too – huge wet shirts and voluminous pairs of trousers draped over bars which were held up by a rope attached to a pulley system.

'DAT BETTER,' said Gorgonzola. 'ALL FRIENDLY, EH? HAVE NICE LITTLE TEA PARTY. NOW DEN. MILK, SUGAR, TEA, BISCUITS, CAKE. WOT HAS ME FORGOT?'

'Nothing, I shouldn't think. It sounds like a real feast.'

'ME SURE ME FORGET SOMETING.' Gorgonzola stood swaying and scratching his head with a puzzled expression. Suddenly, his face cleared. 'HAH! ME REMEMBER!'

'What?'

'CAGE,' said Gorgonzola, with a wicked grin. And he picked up a large kitchen knife, stepped to one side and slashed through the rope that ran up to the rafters.

There was a whistling noise, followed by an almighty

clang – and much to their horror, Dandypants and Jollops found themselves enclosed by bars on all four sides! What Dandypants had assumed to be a system for hanging up wet washing was nothing of the sort. In fact, it was a stout metal cage, about a metre wide and two metres high. The top of the cage was solid steel. Articles of wet clothing, dislodged during the cage's downward flight, lay scattered all over the floor.

'SURPRISED YOU THERE, DIDN'T I?' said Gorgonzola, with a chuckle. Suddenly, he didn't sound *quite* so stupid. 'DIDN'T EXPECT THAT, DID YOU? THOUGHT I WAS DUMB, EH? A POOR, DAFT, OLD GIANT INVITING YOU IN FOR A CUPPA COS I WAS LONELY. WELL, THINK AGAIN, MY LITTLE CHUMS.'

'Now, look here,' said Dandypants, through dry lips. 'I

don't know what you're playing at, but this is hardly sporting, is it? We're just two innocent charity workers collecting hair for the bald and …'

'OH YEAH? AN' I'M THE QUEEN OF THE FAIRIES. TELL ME, MY LITTLE RED FRIEND.' The floor shuddered as he strolled over to the cage and stood looking down at them from his great height. 'DID YOU COME OF YOUR OWN ACCORD? OR DID THE BOSS SEND YOU?'

'Boss? I really don't know what you're talking about. Like I said, we're just collecting hairs for …'

Jollops gave him a nudge.

'Forget it,' he said. 'Ain't it obvious? It's a set-up. He's in the pay of the king.'

'OOOHH!' said Gorgonzola. 'CUTE *AND* CLEVER.'

'What?' said Dandypants. 'I don't quite get what you mean.'

'He's on the king's pay roll,' Jollops explained tiredly. 'King Boris uses him to dispose of people he don't like. Sends 'em off on some tin-pot quest and then they conveniently disappear. Am I right?' he appealed to Gorgonzola, who nodded.

'NEARLY. I DON'T EXACTLY *DISPOSE* OF 'EM.'

'What then?' asked Dandypants.

'WELL, I'M *SUPPOSED* TO KEEP 'EM BANGED UP IN THE CAGE. THAT'S WHAT IT SAYS IN THE CONTRACT. I'M A SORTA JAILER. BUT I'M A GOOD SORT.' Gorgonzola tapped the side of his nose in a meaningful way. 'I'M REASONABLE. IF THEY

PLAYS THEIR CARDS RIGHT, I LETS 'EM OUT FROM TIME TO TIME TO STRETCH THEIR LEGS AND DO A BIT OF SLAVING. LOT O' JOBS NEED DOING AROUND HERE. IT'S SURPRISING HOW HAPPY THEY ARE TO DO A BIT O'COOKING AND WASHING UP AFTER A COUPLA DAYS IN THE CAGE *WITH NO FOOD OR WATER.*'

Gorgonzola gave a triumphant grin and waited to hear how this would go down.

'Well I'm darned,' said Dandypants, thoroughly disgusted. He glared through the bars. 'I'll have you know I'm a *prince*. There is no way — *no way*, under any circumstances — that I'm washing up. I'd sooner rot in here for ever.'

'THEY ALL SAYS THAT,' said Gorgonzola. 'UNTIL THEY GETS HUNGRY.' He walked back to the tray, picked up the entire ginger cake and popped it in his mouth. 'MMM. CAKE. LOVELY. AND NOW I THINK I'LL JUST HAVE TO EAT THESE BISCUITS.'

Dandypants and Jollops watched as he demolished the cake, followed by the tin of biscuits.

'Look,' said Dandypants desperately. 'Surely we can come to some sort of arrangement.'

'I DOUBT IT,' said Gorgonzola, pouring himself a mug of tea.

'But I can pay you.'

'HOW MUCH?'

'Well, I don't have any actual money on me right now, but my father is King Edward of Blott and …'

'FORGET IT. NOT WORTH MY WHILE.'

'And that's your last word on the subject?'

'YEP. OF COURSE, LIKE I SAID, IT DON'T *HAVE* TO BE LIKE THIS. YOU COULD MAKE THINGS EASIER FOR YOURSELVES.'

'How?'

'YOU COULD STOP BEING SO HOITY TOITY, FOR A START. TRY BEING A BIT MORE SOCIABLE. US GIANTS GETS ROTTEN PRESS, BUT WE'RE HUMAN BEINGS, YOU KNOW.' Gorgonzola's voice quavered a little. 'YOU COULD TRY GETTING TO KNOW ME. YOU COULD ASK ME THINGS.'

'Like what?'

'LIKE HOW I AM. HOW I FIND GIANTING. OR

YOU COULD COMPLIMENT ME ON MY HAIR AGAIN LIKE THE LITTLE BROWN ONE DID. CHEER ME UP. THEN I *MIGHT* JUST BEND THE RULES A LITTLE. I MIGHT TAKE PITY ON YOU. AND GIVE YOU SOME SUPPER.'

'Are you serious? *We're* the ones trapped in a cage. You're suggesting *we* cheer *you* up?'

'CORRECT. IT'S A LONG TIME SINCE I HAD A GOOD LAUGH. KNOW ANY GOOD JOKES?'

'No,' said Dandypants tiredly. 'I don't.' Suddenly, it was all too much. His knees gave way and he slithered down the bars to end up with his elbows on his knees and his head in his hands. That it should come to this.

'THAT'S A SHAME. COS IF YOU TOLD ME A JOKE AND MADE ME LAUGH, I MIGHT FEEL DIFFERENTLY ABOUT THINGS. I MIGHT EVEN GIVE YOU THE HAIRS AND SEND YOU ON YOUR WAY.'

'I do,' said Jollops suddenly.

'You do what, Jollops?'

'I know some jokes.'

'HAH!' boomed Gorgonzola. 'GOOD! TELL ME ONE!' Dandypants ignored him.

'No you *don't*, Jollops. You wouldn't know a joke if it came bounding up in a clown's costume and hit you over the head with a tickling stick. You have no sense of humour whatsoever.'

'Yes I do. Look, I wasn't goin' to tell you this, but … well, the fact is, I been doing this course …'

'Course?' Dandypants looked up sharply. 'What course?'

'It's a correspondence course. Fact is, I been study-in' …'

'*Studying?* What? What have you been studying?'

'Jestin',' admitted Jollops. 'I been studying to be a jester.'

'A *jester? You?*'

'Yes.'

'But you're my servant! What gives you the right to … You've kept this from me all this time, and now … A *jester?*'

'Fancied a change,' said Jollops, with a shrug.

'And when do you do this *studying?*'

'Whenever I gets a minute.'

'But you don't *get* a minute, Jollops. Not if you're working for me. You're supposed to be looking after me twenty-four hours a day. And don't tell me about breaks. All break was cancelled when we first set out on this expedition. I made that very clear. What you are doing, Jollops, is studying in *my time.* I take it those are books you've got sneakily stowed away in that stupid sack of yours?'

'Yep.'

'Well I'm darned!' said Dandypants bitterly. 'It comes to something, doesn't it? When a mad giant traps you in a cage…'

'HEY,' said Gorgonzola. 'LESS OF THE MAD.'

'… and tortures you with cake and won't let you out unless you agree to slave for him and then your trusted servant announces he's been secretly studying to be a *jester.*'

'FUNNY OLD LIFE, AIN'T IT? HOW THINGS

WORK OUT,' chipped in Gorgonzola. He had drawn up a chair and was listening in.

'I'll thank you to keep out of this,' snapped Dandypants. 'This is a private conversation between me and my manservant. Jollops, how *dare* you study behind my back? I am ordering you right now to forget this wild dream. You'd make a hopeless jester. You are, quite frankly, the most un-funny person I have ever met.'

'You haven't heard my knock knock joke.'

'And I don't want to.'

'I DO,' said Gorgonzola. He set down his mug with a crash and pointed with a sausage finger at Dandypants. 'I'VE HAD ENOUGH OF YOU, RED ONE. LET THE LITTLE BROWN ONE TELL HIS JOKE.'

'But ...'

'SHUT UP. THAT'S AN ORDER.'

'And if I don't?'

'I'LL POKE YOU WITH A FORK.'

Dandypants shut up.

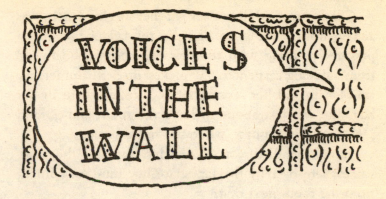

CHAPTER NINETEEN

VOICES IN THE WALL

In which Charlie hears voices and makes
an important discovery.

Charlie stood back and examined the tapestry that now adorned the study wall. She had hung it well, just as Uncle Willard had taught her. It hung straight and was properly secured at the top. All the creases had dropped out. But it did look horribly out of place. Puppies and roses did not belong in this dark, austere room. Still. At least the job was done. All that remained was to pack up her stuff, collect the money and leave.

She glanced through the window. Outside, dusk was falling. Hanging the tapestry had taken longer than she had anticipated, because she was anxious not to damage the panelling more than she had to. She had used the minimum of nails and hammered them in gently in order to avoid splintering the wood.

The castle was very quiet. The builders and decorators

had all gone home and there was no sign of Lady Lushing.

Charlie rubbed the back of her neck, which was aching from looking up. She put the ladder out in the passageway, along with the saw that she had borrowed from a passing carpenter. She picked up her hammer, her tin of nails and her sewing kit and stuffed them in her bag. She was just about to leave the room and go and seek out Lady Lushing when she heard something.

Voices. Muffled voices, filtering through the wall, somewhere over by the tapestry. They must be coming from the room next door.

Except that there *was* no room next door. The study lay behind the last door at the far end of a passageway, she remembered that from when she came in.

And yet there were voices coming through the panelling. How come?

Curious, Charlie set down her bag and walked up to the tapestry. The sounds seemed to come from behind a section of panelling slightly to the left. She stared at the expanse of ancient, polished wood. It was getting dark in the room. She reached out, carefully feeling with the palms of her hands.

It didn't take long to find what she was looking for. A small lever, cunningly concealed in a square of ornate moulding, just above head height. She was surprised she hadn't noticed it before. She had been working within centimetres of it.

She grasped it between thumb and forefinger and eased it down. Instantly, a section of panelling swung away, revealing a small, cupboard like area with a flight of winding steps leading down into darkness below. The voices came from somewhere down there.

There are two kinds of people in the world. If mysterious noises come from downstairs in the middle of the night, there are those who pull the bedclothes over their heads and hope it's the cat and there are those who reach for a big stick and get up to investigate.

Charlie didn't hesitate. She drew her biggest, sharpest knife from her belt – and stepped in.

Lord Lushing was exhausted. For the past few weeks he had been working non-stop. King Boris wasn't the easiest of men to work for. He was always getting bees in his bonnet and coming up with artful ruses and crafty plans that invariably involved Lord Lushing in some unpleasantly active way. Recently, Lord Lushing felt that the king had been, quite frankly, overdoing it. The money was good though, so he didn't say anything. Being clever as well as ambitious, he just did what he was told and reserved all his moaning for Slythe, his trusted valet.

Right now, they were in the Secret Room – a dark, dank, chamber containing little other than a hat stand, a cupboard and a small table, currently awash with important-looking papers, heavily emblazoned with the royal seal. The Secret Room was so secret that even Lord Lushing's wife didn't know it was there. (Just as well. If she had known, she would have painted it pink, put in a fluffy rug and totally ruined its gothic effect.)

The room could be reached in two ways – by stairs from the study, or by way of a long underground tunnel, the entrance of which was cleverly hidden beneath a clump of blackberry bushes some way beyond the castle walls. Lord Lushing could come and go as he pleased without anyone knowing, which came in useful at times. Times like now, when he needed to change quickly into his disguise.

The room also contained a full-length mirror, before which Lord Lushing was standing in his shirt sleeves.

'Pass me the cloak, Slythe,' he sighed. 'Hurry it up, man, I haven't got all night. *Gad,* what I'd do for a good night's sleep in my own bed.'

'Busy night ahead, my lord?' murmured Slythe, passing the cloak with a small bow.

'Alas, yes. Since when *hasn't* it been a busy night? King Boris has a lot of irons in the fire, Slythe. I hardly get a chance to relax these days. I can't remember when I had a weekend off. I haven't seen Sonia for *weeks*. I haven't a clue what she's getting up to. You know how bored she gets when I'm away. Pass me the boots.'

'Ah,' said Slythe. 'I've been meaning to talk to you about that, my lord. There's something I feel you should know. Her ladyship is …'

'What? Pass me the sword belt. Quickly, man quickly. I have many miles to ride tonight.'

'About her ladyship, my lord. She's been …'

'*Gad,* Slythe. Don't bother me with domestic trivia *now*. Don't you think I've got enough on my plate? Whatever she's up to, I just don't want to know, all right? Where's my beard?'

'Right here, lordship.' Slythe passed him a handful of something black and hairy. Lord Lushing looked at it with distaste.

'*Gad,* I hate these whiskers. I'll be glad when this business with Blott is over. Rabble rousing is *not* one of my favourite occupations. Particularly when one is dealing with Blottian peasants. It's going a lot slower than I would like. It's like trying to organize an uprising with a load of exceptionally thick sheep. They can't do anything on their own. They moan a lot and chuck the occasional bit of mud, but that hardly amounts to full-scale revolt, does it? I keep trying to explain this to King Boris, but he's only interested in results. Plus, he's got his mind on other things. Getting the Princess Langoustina married off, for one.'

'And how are the suitor auditions going, sir?' enquired Slythe, carefully applying glue from a small pot on to his master's chin.

'How do you think? Badly. Ouch! Careful, that glue's giving me a rash. And just to complicate matters, guess who turned up to claim her hand this morning?'

'I can't imagine, sir.'

'Prince Daniel of Blott, that's who!'

'Never! What, the one they call Dandypants? King Edward's son?'

'The very same. Turned up bold as you like, despite me organizing the mob to steal his belongings and hang him upside down from a tree.'

'Oh, well done, my lord! What a mastermind you are.'

'Tactics, Slythe, tactics. But thank you. It's good to know that someone appreciates my talents.'

'And young Prince Dandypants didn't put two and two together? He knows nothing of the king's plans, or your involvement?'

'Nothing. He's two peacocks short of a banquet, that one. He even allowed himself to be goaded into choosing −' Lord Lushing paused for dramatic effect − *'The Purple Quest!'*

'Ah,' said Slythe, nodding knowingly. 'The Purple Quest. That involves the Giant Gorgonzola, does it not?'

'Correct. So now I've orders to go and pay *him* off, on top of everything else.'

'Look on the bright side, sir. At least young Prince Dandypants will be kept out of circulation for a while.'

'Let's hope so. I don't want him running around like a loose cannon. Now, if only I can get those wretched peasants to revolt in a proper manner, we'd be getting somewhere. I was rather hoping to get them storming the palace gates by Friday so I could take the weekend off, but that might be pushing it a bit.' His lordship gave another sigh. 'All right, the beard's stuck. Pass me the moustache. And the mask.'

Charlie crouched in shadow at the top of the stairs and tried not to breath. She could hardly take it in. *So the notorious Masked Avenger was none other than Lord Lushing, right-hand man to King Boris of Vulgaria!*

Wonders would never cease.

And what was that about Dandypants and a Giant? Had the idiot got himself into trouble again?

'How do I look?' came his lordship's voice from below.

'Lean, mean and thrillingly sinister, my lord.'

'Good. Well, I'd best get going. I've a hard night's riding to do. I shall call in at the giant's first and get that over and done with, then it's back to the mob in Blott, I suppose. More rousing speeches about justice and all that nonsense. What fools they are to believe in me. I'll leave you to tidy up and put out the candles. And make sure you lock away those documents. They're highly sensitive. We don't want them falling into the wrong hands.'

There came the sound of footsteps moving away.

'Good luck, my lord,' called Slythe. 'Don't you worry, I'll make sure everything's in order. You can trust me, lordship.'

He moved around the tiny room, snuffing out candles

and picking up clothing, which he hung neatly on the hat stand. By the light of the single remaining candle, he gathered together the scattered papers on the table and took them to the cupboard. He took a large key from his pocket and was just about to insert it into the lock, when he noticed an unusual sensation in the small of his back. An unpleasant, pricking sensation.

'Don't move a muscle, Slythe,' breathed a voice in his ears. 'I don't want to hurt you. In fact, I shall shortly let you slither about your business. But first, you and I are going to have a little talk.'

CHAPTER TWENTY

JOKING WITH THE GIANT

*In which Jollops tries out his sense of humour. A surprise
visitor shows up — followed by another!*

'… So the duck looks up to the waiter and says, Put it
on my bill!' finished Jollops.

There was a long silence.

'I DON'T GET THAT ONE EITHER,' said
Gorgonzola.

'*Bill*,' said Jollops. 'He says, Put it on my *bill*. He's a
duck, see.'

'SO WHAT'S HE DOING IN A RESTAURANT?'

'It's a *joke!*' cried Jollops crossly. 'It's a play on
the word *bill*, don't you see? Because he's a *duck*. Look,
I'll run it past you again. This duck goes into a
restaurant …'

'Jollops,' said Dandypants tiredly. 'Give up. Forget it.
It's a rotten joke. All your jokes are rotten. You're a rotten
servant and you'd make an even more rotten jester. And

I still can't believe you'd leave me, after all I've done for you.'

He was sitting on the floor with his back against the bars, cleaning his fingernails with the point of Prince Florentine's sword. He had been cleaning them for what felt like hours while Jollops told jokes. Jokes about doctors and curtains and eggs. Jokes about flies in soup, gooseberries, chickens, elephants and trifle. Knocking-on door jokes. All of them had gone down like a lead balloon. Gorgonzola had a very literal mind. Even when a joke was explained to him several times over, he didn't get it.

'HE'S RIGHT, YOU KNOW,' said Gorgonzola. 'YOUR JOKES *ARE* ROTTEN. AND YOU DON'T TELL 'EM RIGHT. THAT VOICE YOU PUT ON – I LIKED IT TO BEGIN WITH, BUT IT'S GETTING ON MY NERVES NOW.'

'You see?' said Dandypants. 'He agrees with me. Putting on a silly voice doesn't help. It's the material that's at fault. Where do you get your rubbish jokes, Jollops? Out of your stupid *jesting* books?'

'No,' admitted Jollops. 'There's nothin' funny in there, believe me.'

'Where then?'

'Crackers, mostly. And people tells me 'em. In the servants' hall and that.' Jollops sounded sulky. His throat was sore from using his comedy voice. He had dredged up every single joke he could remember, and nobody had even tittered.

'I'VE HEARD ENOUGH JOKES,' said Gorgonzola. 'HOW ABOUT A SING-SONG? KNOW ANY SONGS, LITTLE FELLER?'

156

'I wouldn't go there if I were you,' said Dandypants.

'NO?' Gorgonzola sounded disappointed. 'I LIKES A BIT O' SINGING, I DO. OH WELL. WHAT NEXT? ANYONE PLAY SNAP? IT'S THIS REALLY GOOD CARD GAME ...'

'No,' chorused Dandypants and Jollops together. 'And it's getting late,' added Dandypants. 'I'm starving. Jollops has made me so upset, I could eat a horse. Are you going to give us some supper? Or are you just playing with us?'

'YES.'

'Yes you'll give us some supper?'

'YES I'M JUST PLAYING WITH YOU. AND YOU'RE NOT MUCH FUN. I LIKES MY PRISONERS TO BE FUN. YOU'LL HAVE TO DO BETTER THAN THIS IF YOU WANT TO GET ON MY GOOD SIDE.'

Just then there came a sharp knocking at the front door. Everyone looked startled, including Gorgonzola.

'Open in the name of the king!' came the imperious command.

'AHA,' said Gorgonzola, relaxing. 'GOODY. THAT'LL BE MY BAG OF GOLD. PAYMENT FOR CAPTURING YOU.' He raised his voice even louder. Several cups fell off the draining board and smashed on the floor. 'ALL RIGHT, ALL RIGHT, I'M COMING, I'M COMING.' He pointed a finger. 'YOU STAY HERE LIKE GOOD BOYS. I'LL BE RIGHT BACK.'

And with that, he stomped from the kitchen. In the distance, a door crashed shut. There came the sound of muffled voices, then clomping footsteps returning. There was another set of footsteps as well. Crisp-sounding, booted ones.

The giant once again appeared before them. With him was a familiar figure. Black boots – black cloak – black mask – sardonic smile.

'*You* again!' ground out Dandypants. He leaped to his feet and threw himself against the bars. 'What are you doing here? You ... you rotten *cad*! Turning our own peasants against us!'

'Your highness,' said the Masked Avenger. Coolly, he inclined his head. 'We meet again.'

''Ere! I know that voice,' said Jollops. 'It's that bloke what showed us to the bog. Except he didn't have a beard. That Lord Lushin'!'

'Well-observed,' said Lord Lushing smoothly, with a little smile. 'As your servant has so astutely pointed out, we are indeed, one and the same. I see you put the palace facilities to good use, your highness. I believe Prince Florentine is looking for you. It appears you – what is the phrase? – half inched his clothes.'

'I did,' said Dandypants stiffly. 'Red is not my colour, particularly teamed with green, and the hose are a disaster, but it was an emergency.'

'ENOUGH FASHION TALK,' interrupted Gorgonzola. 'WHERE'S MY GOLD? I WANTS TO COUNT IT.'

Lord Lushing gave an impatient sigh, swished his cloak and tapped the pointed toe of his high-heeled boot.

'Is this really necessary?' he asked. 'I am in rather a hurry. I can assure you there are one hundred gold coins, as agreed. I counted them myself.'

'I WANTS TWO,' said Gorgonzola hopefully. 'ONE HUNDRED FOR EACH PRISONER.'

'Nonsense. One hundred per kidnapping. That was the agreement. Don't be greedy, Gorgonzola. His majesty doesn't like greedy employees. Take the one hundred, or he'll find himself another giant. A bigger one. A *better* one.'

'I STILL WANTS TO COUNT IT,' said Gorgonzola, sulkily. 'THAT'S FAIR.'

'*Gad,* you're stubborn!' Exasperated, Lord Lushing reached below his cloak and withdrew a small sack. He threw it on the kitchen table, causing a small landslide of greasy dishes. 'Count it then, if you must! But be quick about it. I've got people to meet, places to go, plotting to do.'

'Yes!' cried Dandypants, rattling the bars. 'I bet you have, you – you dastardly *scoundrel*, you! You *rotter*! You out and out *blighter*! You *snake in the grass*! You – *naughty*! You – what else shall I call him, Jollops?'

'I think he's got the idea,' said Jollops.

'My, my!' Lord Lushing sounded somewhat amused. 'We *are* upset. I can assure you it's nothing personal, your highness. I'm just doing my job.'

'Some job!' spat Dandypants. 'Some *job*, sneaking into somebody else's kingdom and winding up somebody else's peasants and saying rude things about me and getting my parents all upset! Pops would never have thrown me out if it wasn't for you. It's all *your* fault I'm here! If I wasn't in this cage, I'd give you a jolly good thrashing! Hey! Gorgonzola! Let me out! I want to get at him!'

'ONE,' began Gorgonzola in the background. He was counting gold pieces into a greasy colander. 'TWO – THREE – FOUR ...'

'To some extent, you are right,' agreed Lord Lushing. 'I certainly stirred public opinion against you. That, I own up to. But I was hardly to know that you would come claiming Langoustina's hand. That complicated matters somewhat.'

'But, *why*?' wailed Dandypants. 'What's the point of it all?'

'NINE – TEN – TEN AND ONE – TEN AND TWO ...'

'*Please!*' snapped Lord Lushing, glaring over his

shoulder at Gorgonzola. His silky voice was fraying somewhat at the edges. 'Keep it *down* over there, would you? We're trying to talk here.' He turned again to Dandypants. 'Where was I again?'

'Unveiling your vile, wicked plan.'

'ONE – TWO – THREE …'

'Ah yes. Well, it's quite simple, your highness. King Boris is determined to overthrow your father and add Blott to his list of conquests. It's a sort of – personal challenge. There is quite a bit of animosity between him and your father arising from some sort of Playground Incident regarding tuck, or possibly conkers. Who knows? Who cares? The details are lost in the mists of time. Whatever it was, King Boris is very keen to get his own back. Unfortunately, some rule prevents fellow St Aloofees …'

'SEVEN – EIGHT – NINE …'

'All right, all right, I know all about that,' chipped in Dandypants. 'This is all old family history. I've heard it from Pops a million times. Belcher Boris can't come marching in and taking us over by force out of respect for the old school tie and fear of The Old Headmaster. And quite jolly right too.'

'Indeed. But there is nothing to prevent him from whipping up a rebellion from *within*.'

'TEN – TEN AND ONE …'

'Keep it down, I say!'

'STOP SHOUTING AT ME THEN. I KEEPS FORGETTING WHERE I AM.'

'Ah. I *see*. In other words, our own peasants will do his dirty work for him, yes? They'll rise up and drive us out from the palace, leaving the throne vacant for him to sneak in and park his fat backside on, yes? Yes? Is that what this is all about?'

'ONE – TWO –THREE …'

'You have it in a nutshell. Count *quietly*, Gorgonzola, can't you?'

'FOUR – FIVE – SIX …'

'Well,' said Dandypants. 'I'm disgusted. Of all the sneaky, underhand things to do. You wait till Pops hears about this. There'll be trouble at the next old boys reunion, mark my words. The Old Headmaster won't like this. Old St Aloofians have very strong ideas about this sort of thing. Questions will be asked. I wouldn't be in Boris's shoes. There might be a public reprimand. There might be *detention*.'

'TEN AND ONE – TEN AND TWO –'

'Mmmmm.' Lord Lushing stroked his false beard thoughtfully. 'Do you know, I think *not*. Nobody knows the identity of the Masked Avenger except for your good self. And *you're* not going anywhere, are you?'

'You make me sick, you do!' raged Dandypants. 'Pretending you're on the side of the peasants when really you're just using them for your own ends. That's – what's that's word again? Begins with an X?'

'Xylophone?' suggested Jollops.

'No! Exploitation!'

'Oh, come, come, your highness!' Lord Lushing raised an amused eyebrow. 'That's rich, coming from *your* lips. You haven't given a hoot about the peasants until now, although their taxes put the clothes on your back. Why all this outrage?'

'He's got a point there,' said Jollops.

'TWO TENS AND ONE – TWO TENS AND TWO –'

'Maybe you're right,' said Dandypants stiffly. 'But I don't make the rules. It's Pops that runs the country, not me. The fact remains that they're *our* peasants. *Our* country, *our* peasants. Belcher Boris has got no right to meddle in our affairs.'

'Face facts. He has. And quite frankly, *Prince Dandypants*, there is nothing you can do about it. Now, you really must excuse me. Tonight, I ride to Blott. It isn't easy turning a rabble of milkmaids and straw-hatted pitchfork-wielders into an army. I have my work cut out. But I'm getting there. We've covered burning, now we're moving on to rude graffiti, gratuitous chanting and throwing rocks through windows. Your clothes, by the way, made an excellent bonfire. Your mother in particular was most upset to see them go up in flames. She came running out with a bucket of water. You father had to hold her back. Rumour has it she sleeps with one of your charred hats.'

'*Swine!*' raged Dandypants, rattling the bars. 'You won't get away with this! The word will get out, you'll see! People will suspect.'

'Possibly. But King Boris will deny everything. What is suspicion without proof?'

Crash!

Suddenly, the world was full of flying glass. Gorgonzola gave a bellow of surprise and leapt to his feet, overturning the colander. Gold coins rolled all over the floor. Dandypants and Jollops threw themselves to the floor and covered their heads as glass and coins pinged against the cage bars. Lord Lushing, with a muttered curse, whirled around, his hand automatically going for his rapier.

The window over the sink was no more. Instead, there was a gaping hole through which the night air blew. And there, crouched on the window sill, was a slight, boyish figure holding a bow with a cocked arrow that pointed unwaveringly at Lord Lushing.

'Don't try it, if you know what's good for you,' said Charlie. 'Get your hands up. Now.'

CHAPTER TWENTY-ONE

THE FINAL SHOWDOWN

In which the Masked Avenger is unmasked and Jollops's
text books come in useful.

'Well, now,' said Lord Lushing. Slowly, he raised his
hands. 'It appears we have company. And who might you
be, lad? Do I know you?'

'The name's Charlie Tuffgrissel and I'm a girl, not a
lad.' Lightly, she jumped down on to the floor, still
keeping the arrow trained on Lord Lushing. 'No you
don't know me. But I know all about you and your nasty
little games. Your Secret Room's not as secret as you
think. You really shouldn't leave sensitive documents
lying around.'

Lord Lushing went pale beneath his mask.

'You mean …?'

'I mean I've got a whole pile of private
correspondence from King Boris to you. Instructions,
dates, everything. All the proof we need. And I had a

interesting little chat with your valet before I followed you here. I know everything you and the king have been up to.'

'Hah!' shouted Dandypants. 'You see? Didn't expect that, did you?'

Lord Lushing's mouth twisted in a grimace of rage.

'Gorgonzola!' he rapped. 'Do something! Now!'

All this time, Gorgonzola had been staring from one to the other with his mouth open. There was just that bit too much plot for him to take in. He was still trying to come to terms with the fact that his gold was spilled and that his kitchen window was currently lying in shards all over the floor.

'WHA?' he said.

'*Do* something, fool. You're big enough. *Get her!*'

'I wouldn't, Gorgonzola,' said Charlie steadily. Her eyes never left Lord Lushing's face. 'Move a finger, and Lushing gets it. We don't want to make even more of a mess of your floor, do we?'

'All right, all right!' said Lord Lushing hastily. '*Don't* get her. Do whatever she says.'

'Sensible man. Right. Here's what you do, Gorgonzola. You raise that cage and release the prisoners.'

'And jolly well hurry up about it!' added Dandypants. He felt slightly put out. It was a big relief that they were being rescued, of course, but the cage put him at a disadvantage. He felt he should be out there, waving his sword around and generally being part of the action.

Gorgonzola gave a shrug, reached up, grabbed the dangling rope and pulled. The cage went rattling up into the shadows, and Dandypants and Jollops were free at last!

'Right,' said Dandypants, striding up to Lord Lushing and poking him hard in the chest. 'It's all different now, isn't it? The tables have finally turned. So I'm a pampered hanger-on, am I? Make fun of my name, would you? Care to do it again?'

'Get back, idiot,' warned Charlie. 'You're in the way. I haven't got a clear …'

What happened next took everyone by surprise. Lord Lushing suddenly brought his raised arms down and gave Dandypants a violent push. Dandypants staggered backwards, arms wheeling wildly, and collided directly

with Charlie, knocking her bow from her hand. Both of them went crashing to the floor. The released arrow flew towards the ceiling where it stuck, quivering.

Lord Lushing wasted no time. He gathered his cloak around him, vaulted the sink and was out the broken window and away before anyone could stop him!

That left only the giant to contend with.

'HAH!' roared Gorgonzola, striding towards Dandypants and Charlie, who were desperately trying to untangle themselves on the floor. He bent down, his huge hands reaching for them. 'NOW I GOT YOU! I TEACH YOU TO BREAK MY WINDOW AND SPILL MY GOLD.'

'And I'll teach you not to laugh at my jokes,' said Jollops from behind him. He had hold of his sack full of books and was spinning it around by the drawstring. As Gorgonzola turned his huge head, he let fly.

Thwock! The sack whizzed through the air, connecting sharply with Gorgonzola's forehead. The giant looked momentarily surprised. Then his eyes came over all glazed, and with a little sigh, he pitched forward and landed on the floor with a huge thump, missing Dandypants and Charlie by centimetres.

They sat up and looked from Jollops to the collapsed giant, then back again.

'Wow!' said Charlie, after a long, shocked silence. 'Heavy reading!'

'Well done, Jollops,' said Dandypants. 'I must say, I am pleasantly surprised. For once, you came up trumps.'

'Yeah, yeah,' growled Jollops. But he looked pleased.

'What shall we do about Lord Lushing? Shouldn't we

race off in hot pursuit?' asked Dandypants. 'We can't let
him get away with this.'

'Let him go,' said Charlie. 'He'll be punished enough
when he sees what his wife's done to his castle.' She
looked at their uncomprehending faces and grinned.
'Come on. I'll tell you all about it on the way home.'

CHAPTER TWENTY-TWO

HOME AGAIN

*In which some wrongs – not all – are righted and
Queen Hilda loses the plot.*

'… And then we came home,' finished Dandypants triumphantly. He reached out and took a big swig of orange juice. He had been talking for some time. There had been a lot of ground to cover. His throat was quite sore.

'So I take it you won't be marrying Princess Langoustina?' said Queen Hilda, sounding rather disappointed.

'Not jolly likely. Honestly, Mumsy, you wouldn't have liked her. I think she was quite keen on me, but she just wasn't my type.'

'But I thought that was the whole point of you going away. To get a bride.'

'Of course he can't marry her,' said King Edward irritably. 'What are you thinking of, Hilda? She's Belcher

Boris's daughter. The man's been plotting to overthrow me! It's all here.' He indicated the pile of letters and documents laid out before him on the breakfast table. 'Plain as a pike staff.'

'Not to me, it isn't,' said Queen Hilda, helping herself to a muffin. 'In fact, I find it all rather confusing. I understand that the Masked Avenger turned out to be Lord Lashing …'

'Lushing,' Dandypants corrected her.

'… Lushing, yes, sorry, darling, it's rather a lot of names to take in, isn't it? Lord Lushing, who you say is King Boris's right-hand man, but what was Willard Tuffgrissel's niece, what's her name …'

'Charlie. It's short for Charlene.'

'… Yes, Charlie, what was she doing at his wife's castle? And what was all that strange business with the giant's hair? I didn't quite *get* that bit. And why is your dwarf studying to be a jester?'

'Well, you see …'

'Never mind, darling, I'm not terribly good at plots. Please don't go over it again. I'm sure it all turned out for the best, and it's lovely to have you home. Pass the butter.'

'Well,' said King Edward, folding his reading glasses. 'I must say, you've done well, son. These documents establish Belcher Boris's guilt beyond the shadow of a doubt. I shall present them to The Old Headmaster at the Old Boy's reunion next week. There will be repercussions. Oh dear me, yes. I'd go so far as to say there will be a ceremonial removal of the old school tie. Oh, the disgrace! He's really in for it this time. I can't wait.' He gave a schoolboyish snigger.

'Of course, you could handle it another way, Pops,' said Dandypants thoughtfully.

'Eh? How d'you mean?'

'Well, I was chatting to Charlie quite a bit on the way home. And Jollops too, actually. I must say, they got me thinking.'

'Thinking? Thinking about what?'

'About the way the country is run. In a way, you can't blame the peasants for feeling a bit hard done by. They may not have a leader any more, but they're still far from happy. Coming back through Skwallor was no picnic, I can tell you. The Masked Avenger did his job well. There were stones mixed in with the mud this time, and I noticed that their pitchfork waving is a lot more co-ordinated. And have you noticed the graffiti on the palace gates? The problem's not going away, Pops. Perhaps – this is just a thought, mind – perhaps, just as an experiment, you could try a different approach.'

'*A different approach?*'

'Here's a novel idea. Well, actually, it's Charlie's, but it's a jolly good one. What if you cancel Tax Day this year?'

'*What?* Are you *mad*?'

'No, listen. I have to be frank here, Pops. I know your feelings about Belcher Boris being a nasty piece of work, but I must say that Vulgaria is – well, not so *uncomfortable* as Blott. It's a fairer system. Everyone looks a lot more cheerful. They pay taxes, of course, but only a proportion of what they earn. And in return, they get cobbled streets and decent houses and reasonably priced restaurants and water pumps and stuff. Interesting idea, isn't it? I thought we might copy it.'

'*Copy?*' cried the king. 'Copy old Belcher's way of doing things? That's it! The boy's finally flipped!'

'Sssh, dear,' said Queen Hilda. 'Listen to him. Go on, darling.'

'It's just that King Boris knows how to keep his subjects happy. It makes sense, doesn't it? Keeping people happy? He is quite popular, you know. Wouldn't you like to be popular? I mean, it's much better to be cheered than booed, isn't it?'

'He has a point, you know, darling,' said the queen.

'You see?' said Dandypants. 'Mumsy agrees. Now, here's an idea. Well, it's another one of Charlie's, but just let me run it by you. Instead of Tax Day, we throw a huge party for all the peasants in the palace grounds. Music, dancing, baked potatoes, games, jugglers, bonfire, fireworks, the lot.'

'Have you any idea how much that would co …'

'Wait, wait, hear me out. At the end, you stand up and make a speech. You promise to build them their houses and hospital and school and all the rest of it, including getting the pump fixed. And then – here's the masterstroke – *you actually do it!* Just think how much they'll love you.'

'But the cost!' cried King Edward, horrified. 'The *cost!*'

'Ah,' said Dandypants. 'But the beauty of it is, you won't have to pay for it. Not one penny.'

'I won't?'

'No.'

'Then who will?'

'King Boris,' said Dandypants simply. 'He can afford it. You get him to cough up for the lot, on pain of exposure at the next reunion. If he agrees to pick up the tab, you let him off the hook and no more will be said. If he refuses, you go ahead and present all the evidence to The Old Headmaster.'

'That's blackmail,' said the king, after a longish pause.

'Ooh,' said Queen Hilda. 'How thrilling!'

'Exactly,' said Dandypants. 'We've got him cornered, Pops. What do you say?'

King Edward thought about this. 'Clever,' he said finally. 'Very crafty and clever. Son, you have more brains than I credited you for.'

'Actually, that was Charlie's idea too,' admitted Dandypants, after a brief struggle with his conscience. 'But I think it's a good one.'

'So there we are then,' trilled Queen Hilda. 'All sorted. Well done, darling. I think this calls for a rise in his allowance, don't you, Teddy? For some new clothes. Unless he wants to donate it to the peasants, of course. Now he's on their side.'

'No,' said Dandypants darkly. 'They strung me up by my heels and set my clothes on fire. I'm darned if I'm going that far.'

Some time later, Jollops and Charlie sat on the five-barred gate, watching Dandypants fail miserably at his archery lesson.

'No, sir,' Willard was saying patiently. 'Sight along the arrow. Don't look at your shoes.'

'You mean, like this?'

'No, no. Look, you're not holding it right …'

'Doesn't improve, does he?' said Jollops to Charlie. She had Stuart in her arms, and was stroking his long, silky ears.

'No,' said Charlie. 'He's stopped slapping his thigh though. That's something. By the way, how's the correspondence course going?'

'Given it up. Made me too miserable, bein' funny. Besides –' Jollops gave a little sigh – 'besides, someone's got to look after him.'

There came the twang of released string, and another arrow plopped harmlessly into the stream.

'I think I'm getting the hang of it now!' shouted Dandypants. 'Did you see that one, Tuffgrissel? That was my best yet. I think I'll quit, while I'm on a roll.'

As he came bounding towards them, the sun came out.

And that is as happy an ending as you're going to get.

For those readers who like to see things neatly tied up, here are the answers to your questions.

Did King Boris pay up? Yes. Reluctantly.

How did the feast go? Brilliantly. King Edward's speech was very well received. Several peasants sidled up to Dandypants and gruffly apologized for picking on him, before rushing off to get stuck into the sausages.

Did Charlie wear a dress? No.

What did Dandypants wear? Pale-blue velvet doublet, matching hose in the correct size, and a fabulous pair of boots.

Who did Princess Langoustina marry? No one. King Boris gave up on her and bought her a hairdressing salon called Hair to the Throne.

What about Gorgonzola? He came round eventually. It took days to find all the gold pieces. When he finally got it all together, he bought himself a pair of seven league boots, closed the Big House and went travelling. He had a lot of good adventures and didn't have to clear up the kitchen.

And Lord Lushing? He saw what his wife had done to the castle. He's staying home a lot more these days.

What happened at the next Old Boy's reunion? King Edward and King Boris bowed stiffly to each other, enquired after each other's wives and then moved on as if nothing had happened.

What *was* the Playground Incident? Ah. Some things you never find out.

Read more in Puffin

For complete information about books available from Puffin – and Penguin – and how to order them, contact us at the appropriate address below. Please note that for copyright reasons the selection of books varies from country to country.

www.puffin.co.uk

In the United Kingdom: Please write to **Dept EP, Penguin Books Ltd,
Bath Road, Harmondsworth, West Drayton, Middlesex UB7 ODA**

In the United States: Please write to **Penguin Putnam Inc., P.O. Box 12289,
Dept B, Newark, New Jersey 07101–5289 or call 1–800–788–6262**

In Canada: Please write to **Penguin Books Canada Ltd,
10 Alcorn Avenue, Suite 300, Toronto, Ontario M4V 3B2**

In Australia: Please write to **Penguin Books Australia Ltd,
P.O. Box 257, Ringwood, Victoria 3134**

In New Zealand: Please write to **Penguin Books (NZ) Ltd,
Private Bag 102902, North Shore Mail Centre, Auckland 10**

In India: Please write to **Penguin Books India Pvt Ltd,
11 Panscheel Shopping Centre, Panscheel Park, New Delhi 110 017**

In the Netherlands: Please write to **Penguin Books Netherlands bv,
Postbus 3507, NL–1001 AH Amsterdam**

In Germany: Please write to **Penguin Books Deutschland GmbH,
Metzlerstrasse 26, 60594 Frankfurt am Main**

In Spain: Please write to **Penguin Books S. A., Bravo Murillo 19,
1° B, 28015 Madrid**

In Italy: Please write to **Penguin Italia s.r.l.,
Via Felice Casati 20, I–20124 Milano**

In France: Please write to **Penguin France S. A.,
17 rue Lejeune, F–31000 Toulouse**

In Japan: Please write to **Penguin Books Japan, Ishikiribashi Building,
2–5–4, Suido, Bunkyo-ku, Tokyo 112**

In South Africa: Please write to **Longman Penguin Southern Africa (Pty) Ltd,
Private Bag X08, Bertsham 2013**